TRUTH, LOVE AND LIES

Florence Swan's plan is to escape from Benford Mill School for young women before she is forced to work in their cotton mill. Naïve, ambitious and foolhardy, she ventures out on her own, her path crossing that of Mr Luke Stainbridge — a man accused of being mad. He has returned home from imprisonment in France to discover that his home has been claimed by an impostor. Together they find the truth, disproving clever lies, and discover life anew.

VALERIE HOLMES

◆

TRUTH, LOVE AND LIES

Complete and Unabridged

LINFORD
Leicester

First published in Great Britain in 2010

First Linford Edition
published 2011

British Library CIP Data

Holmes, Valerie.
  Truth, love and lies. - -
  (Linford romance library)
  1. Love stories.
  2. Large type books.
  I. Title II. Series
  823.9′2–dc22

  ISBN 978–1–4448–0848–3

Published by
F. A. Thorpe (Publishing)
Anstey, Leicestershire

Set by Words & Graphics Ltd.
Anstey, Leicestershire
Printed and bound in Great Britain by
T. J. International Ltd., Padstow, Cornwall

This book is printed on acid-free paper

1

The room fell silent. Each girl stopped working as Mrs Haggerty angrily entered the dormitory where they worked and slept. Again she shouted out the name of one of the older girls.

'Florence Swan!'

All eleven girls resumed their work — the delicate business of mending or making lace on their cushions which were covered with systematically placed pins, with bobbin, spindle or needles in busy hands — as Mrs Haggerty stormed in, quickly striding down the lines of wooden desks until she came to the one where no work was being done. She glared at the two most senior girls at either side of the empty bench chair.

Thwack! The birch came down on the unused table, the sound reverberating from the stone walls. 'Where is Swan?' She turned, scanning the heads of the other females as if trying to find a target to pick on.

All the other girls looked down, praying she would not single them out. All had felt the sting of the birch at one time or another; however, no one knew where Florence was.

This was how Florence had planned it; she had learned early in life that only if a secret was not shared, could it not be divulged. Her plan had been carefully worked out; once Florence had committed her feet to running away and hiding on the stores barge, which passed down river after emptying its load at the mill school, her destiny was to run. She would live a life beyond an itchy grey uniform, a loveless existence between cold stone walls — and avoiding Mrs Haggerty's birch.

By the time Mrs Haggerty had alerted Mr Jakes, the Parish Beadle of the mill, that a girl had absconded, Florence Swan was already twenty miles away — and free.

Florence lay on her back staring at the stars above. It was a clear night and quite warm; the ground was not so kind to her as she lay there, cuddling her small sack bag that contained all she owned, but then it was earth and Florence expected that it would be cold.

She had planned her escape months ago, and had waited until she managed to mend an old coat that had been discarded near the rag bin in the yard of the school. No one had seen it there, so no one knew she had taken it, but from that one chance find, Florence had hatched her plan.

The weather was warm and her date of transfer to the mill was approaching, but she had no intention of going to a mill, for she had been told about life in them by Jake the delivery boy who fetched the cotton and flax on the barge. Florence had more faith in his words than the lies of Haggerty, for he had been there and seen the place. The dirt, smoke and long hours aged people beyond their years.

Florence had then begun to share this information with one of the other girls, Molly. But Molly had been so scared by it that, without thinking of the possible consequences, she had run straight to Mrs Haggerty. That was why Florence had been warned so firmly about spreading 'evil lies' under the threat of a birching.

No, Florence Swan was going to have a life of her own — she had plans for a future where she would run her own workshop and sell lace to fine ladies, until she could afford to become one herself.

So she lay in the shelter of a fallen tree and stared at the stars. Tomorrow she would walk to a fine house, one of the small manor houses that littered the county. There she would ask about employment and hope that she could disappear from the outside world into its kitchens as a lowly maid.

While working there, she would be able to eat her fill and hopefully, before too long, also earn enough coin for a fare to the city, and from there she would start her new life. For now, though, she slept, breathed fresh air and continued to dream her dreams.

★   ★   ★

Luke was hungry, but he was also anxious to return to his beautiful home. It had been a long journey by packet from London to Whitby. From there he had accepted a lift upon a wagon to the edge of the moor. He had walked down the old track which crossed the moor carrying a pack, spurred on because he could not wait to see his cousin again.

He had thought of sending a message ahead of him, but could not put into words what he felt. The shock might be too much for Archibald, who had always been of a more sensitive composure, so Luke decided he would arrive and the very fact that he was there in person, alive, would say it all.

Many nights in a dark prison had almost deprived him of his sanity, let alone any hope of ever returning to the shores of his homeland in anything resembling good health. If it had not been for the kindness of one Frenchman, he could have starved or died of fever in a foreign land, forgotten by his country, listed as one more lost soul, missing or presumed killed while fighting for King and country.

He had run the scene through his mind many times. His cousin would welcome him in the hall, delighted to see him alive. Five years his senior, Archibald would have taken over the running of the manor whilst he had been missing, but now they would be able to share the load and he would never leave England's shores again.

Archibald had not been able to serve his country as he had a lame leg, the result of a hunting accident in his prime. He would have died in spirit by simply witnessing the war. Archibald was a student of the arts; he could not have stomached the bloodshed that Luke had seen.

Luke sighed. Seeing his idealistic cousin would be a tonic — better than any spa water. With this thought in mind, Luke climbed the last rise and saw his home nestled in the vale below the moor. It had taken him time, energy and money to return to his own land. All he had to do now was to present himself at his own door and await a warm and rapturous welcome.

★　★　★

Luke felt as though he had taken an age to walk the long drive to the large colonnaded doorway of the manor he had grown up in — well, during the summers at least. Winters had been spent in the city of York. He rested his hand on the familiar column and could have sunk down there, weeping with relief as he stared at his own land, overwhelmed by being home.

Still, he was a soldier and would not allow himself to crumble emotionally out of happiness, when he had never given in when pushed to the ends of his own despair. He lifted the heavy knocker and let it fall against the door.

It took only a few moments for the handle to turn. He wiped his hand down his jacket quickly to disperse the dust and mud from his sleeve and stood with shoulders back and head held proud, as he prepared to take control of his life once more, returning to his heritage.

The door opened and a servant he did not recognise stood before him in a yellow liveried uniform with white piping upon his epaulettes. The man glared at him.

'Good day,' Luke said, and smiled.

'Who are you and what do you want?' the man asked.

'I am Mr Luke Stainbridge and I want to enter my home, have a soak in a warm tub and meet my cousin, Archibald — not necessarily in that order.' Luke made to step inside, but the man half closed the door and blocked him from moving forward.

'Cooper!' the man shouted and was instantly accompanied by a younger, fitter house servant. 'This man is quite mad. Grab him, whilst I go and fetch the master!'

Luke was tired and bemused. The younger man roughly took hold of his arm. Luke was a soldier, he reacted as any threatened one would do; he fought back. Rage welled inside of him; he was exhausted and battle-weary, but this was his home. Why should he have to fight anyone here?

Soon more hands restrained him until he found himself dragged face down onto the tiled hallway that he had so long dreamed of seeing — though not as close as this.

'Still him! If he struggles, use the master's stick and club him.'

Luke ceased to move.

'That's better, lad. You wait until the master comes. He'll know what to do with you,' the man who held his head whispered in his ear. 'Don't do you any good to go making wild accusations about being someone above yourself. Been at war, eh? Does things to you, don't it? All that noise going off around you and the blood and killing. Many a good man has cracked bad with it. You keep still and quiet like.'

As soon as Luke saw Archibald, he reasoned, all would be explained and then he would dismiss these arrogant wretches or make them work the land bare-handed for a week, until his temper abated.

He had never run from a battle in his life, nor let his men down. They in turn had shown him every respect. Luke was enraged by the insult on top of this appalling attack on his person. People would be punished for this.

It seemed ages before a figure appeared at the top of the stairs. His stairs. The man looked familiar — not unlike himself in build and colouring, and the severity of the expression upon his face. Luke hoped the similarity ended there. He had no right to be on his stairs — and wearing his gown.

'Who is this man?' the strange gentleman asked in an aloof manner.

'He claims to be ... ' The man-servant paused.

'Who? I don't like wretches straddled across my floor!'

'Your floor!' Luke shouted, only to be cuffed about the head for his spontaneous outburst.

'He claims to be Mr Luke Stainbridge, sir. He stood before me as bold as brass and declared it — wants to use your bath and even mentioned poor old Mr Archibald.'The gentleman's face coloured.

'Who are you?' he shouted, but came no closer to Luke.

The grip on Luke's arms was slackened. 'More to the point, who are you?' he answered, but this time his question was greeted with a boot landing in his side.

'Manners!' the owner of the boot commanded.

'I am Mr Luke Stainbridge and you are obviously ill or mad, or both.'

This complete stranger declared himself by his name but still he kept his distance. Luke's head was spinning with confusion and disbelief. Had he fallen into a deep sleep in a cold cell in France? Was he still there and living out his worst nightmare?

'Lock him in one of the store rooms and then send for someone from the asylum at Gorebeck. Tell them what has happened and ask them to take him away for examination. Be quick about it. I do not wish to have a lunatic in my home any longer than I have to.' The man turned his back to Luke and began making his way back to his upper landing.

'You know I speak the truth! Who are *you* is the question that needs an answer!' Luke shouted out, to be greeted again by another kick before he was dragged to his feet and along the servants' passage to the kitchens. The gentleman had not answered him or even looked back.

They opened the door to store room and threw him insid

'Where are Marsden, Jenkins, N Ellen and — '

'Never heard of them,' one servant said. 'I'll send food in to you.'

The door was slammed shut, and darkness was Luke's only companion once more. He swallowed, but he did not weep, for his anger was so great. Somehow he had to escape and find out who this impostor was. Where was Archibald? If he could find him, he could unravel this riddle. Until then, he would sleep as best he could, as experience had taught him that without rest and strength there was no hope. Luke always nurtured hope.

★　★　★

Florence saw the manor house along the vale, nestled in front of a forested bank which led up to the moor above. Inner feelings of excitement tinged with st a little fear bubbled up inside her. The river flowed quickly cutting along the vale before disappearing through the woodland; it flowed towards an unseen destination and so, Florence knew, must she. She had seen one man enter through the large doors at the front.

In her hand she held the letter she hoped would help her achieve a position within the house. It was only until she would earn a few shillings and let the trail of her disappearance go cold — then she would move on to a better life. The letter had been written on a sheet of paper she had filched from the beadle's office. She had copied the words from one he had written for a girl who was about to leave for a place in a house. She had been picked out by a gentleman who had come to the mill school. Florence had not envied her, although it had been said she had been blessed with a better life. Florence had taken an instant dislike to the gentleman.

After this employment had served its purpose, she would make her way to the city and to the houses where the fine folk lived and she, Florence Swan, would learn their ways. Florence imagined how she would watch the way they held themselves — studying their manners and speech.

Jake's description of life in a big mill, the dust and long hours, the noise of the looms and the menace of overseers, had filled her with terror; she was determined she was not for that.

Florence looked at the big doors ahead of her. Seeing the way a casual caller was being unceremoniously taken inside, she decided she would be better off going to the servants' quarters at the back.

The hastily written reference was not very good, but it was an improvement on having nothing. She was only trying to find a position as a lowly scullery or laundry maid, after all, not a house-keeper, so they wouldn't expect really posh references, would they?

Excitement and nerves were starting to get the better of her. She made her way around the back of the building, in awe of the size of the place. To her the stable block alone looked like a miniature palace — not that she had seen one before, but it even had its own bell tower. She stopped and stared at it, then the little church to the back of the main house.

Someone was walking around the outskirts of the old building so Florence stepped out of sight, following the line of the main building. A noise came from inside an open door ahead of her. Instantly, Florence reacted to her instincts, guilt swept through her just for being there.

She stepped to the side of the doorway, leaning against the wall so she was in the shadow of the door-frame. Florence was so used to dodging trouble by avoiding Mrs Haggerty that it was second nature to her to hide when she was where she ought not to be. For some reason, despite her intention to be bold and make her presence known, she felt as if she should hide — she sensed that she was in the wrong place.

The voices of the two men resounded down a stone corridor leading to the doorway and the open cobbled yard next to where she was standing. Florence knew should probably make herself known, but there was something about the tone of their voices that prevented her doing so.

'Fancy him turning up like that!' the older man said.

'He'll wish he hadn't come back when they get him to the lunatic asylum. By the time they've done with him, his brains won't know where he is or what he's about. Still, it's not our problem, is it? We're paid to do our jobs and that's what we're doing, like any good servant should. It's not our place to ask questions. Mind, I wonder where he's been all these years.'

'Too right, young Seth. You keep to that and you'll go far. The master rewards loyalty. Don't ask no questions and you learn no lies!'

'Tell you what I do fancy, Mr Jacobs,' he said cheerfully.

'What's that lad?'

'A jug of porter!'

'Aye, why not? The master will be asleep for some time. I'll tell Sally to take the bloke some bread and ale then I'll meet you over there.'

One of the men walked straight out into the yard and crossed to the stable; the other followed another corridor, which Florence presumed led to the kitchen where this Sally would be.

As soon as they had disappeared from view she slipped inside the hall, making her way back from where they had come. If the kitchen was the other way then that, she realised, was where she should go and enquire about the prospect of work.

But she didn't.

Instead, Florence crept along, not really understanding what she was doing or why. She followed the corridor

18

where the men had appeared from. Who, she wondered, had they been talking about?

She hated the feeling of being trapped, and realised that they were keeping someone here, waiting to be hauled away to an asylum. It was none of her business who that was, but she could not help herself; she had to know more. She had credited herself with a good ear for knowing when folk were not acting as they should be. She sensed trouble and prayed that it was not a personal prediction of where she was about to find herself — deep in her own.

Some moments later she was faced with a number of doors set deep within a stone wall, and she did not know what to do. Then she heard footsteps approaching behind her. Not the heavy ones of the men, but lighter quicker ones. Florence ducked into the first of the rooms to find herself surrounded by shelves stacked with cheeses; the smell was overpowering, but leaving the door slightly ajar she watched a maid go by with a wooden platter.

The wench turned the key in the door at the end of the corridor and quickly slipped the tray inside on the floor. As she tried to shut the door firmly someone grabbed it from inside, and she was too slow to react. A hand grabbed her arm, pulling her bodily inside the room. She screamed, but in the time it takes to blink, a man appeared outside in the corridor.

Florence watched him close and lock the door. The girl started to pound on the opposite side, but it was solid and her attempts did not move it. The man looked around. Florence saw his face clearly. He did not strike her as a mad man, more like one who was extremely vexed.

He could have hurt the maidservant to silence her, but he had not. Instead he started to run towards the upper house. Florence also ran; she followed him because she realised the girl's cries would be heard in the corridor and the men would find her if she retraced her steps toward the yard. Whatever he was, Florence decided, he was not a violent man.

She hesitated before leaving the servants' quarters, stepping onto the tiled floor of the hall. Florence saw the man run up the stairs two at a time; he seemed to know where he was going. She saw that he was strong by the way he moved and confident in his stride. As soon as he disappeared onto the upper landing she followed after him.

Florence did not stop to think; she was a creature of instinct. She saw him pause by the double doors to the right of the stairs. Downstairs there was still no sign of the male servants who had incarcerated him. They must have still been in the stables drinking, but who else was in the house she had no idea.

Florence tiptoed toward the door of the bedchamber which he had just entered. On the top step she paused long enough to look up at the painting overhead. She had never seen such a thing of beauty before. She wanted to study it and work out what the old bearded man in the centre of the dome was pointing at, but she had no time to puzzle it out, nor what the escapee was doing. Those questions did not cross her thoughts; she could not stop. She just had to know what was happening, and why.

2

Florence stared through the door jamb and saw the man she had followed standing over another man lying peacefully in his bed. He placed one hand around the man's neck and the other over his mouth.

She stifled a gasp.

'Quiet!' the stranger whispered to the man who was prone before him. 'Tell me who you are and what game you play with me, or I will finish your pretence, here and now, with my bare hands.' He stared down at the surprised figure. He kept his hand on the man's throat, but slowly removed the one covering the gentleman's lips.

'My men will find you, wherever you run,' the man answered calmly.

'Not in time to save you,' the stranger said quickly.

'You are lost, you have no name now.

You should have stayed in France. Admit defeat, and go. Don't force me to have you condemned as a madman. Leave with your life; it is all you have left — enjoy it, whilst you can. You cannot harm me, I have the deeds to this estate, I have been accepted by those who thought they knew me years ago before you ran away to fight and play soldiers.'

The stranger lifted the man by his shoulders. 'I will drag you before the magistrate. You will repeat what you have said before the law of the land!'

'You would have difficulty there, because I am the magistrate and I run the local group of militia. Hurt me, and it will be the gallows that will greet you. Look at yourself in the glass. You are changed from the boy who went away. You should have returned when you were in London, but no, you chose to stay in town and were then sent back to rot in a French gaol. You should have stayed lost.'

'Who are you?' The stranger shook

the man before throwing him back onto the bed.

Florence peered to try to see the impostor's face. She thought he was smiling. 'You will go to your grave wondering that, Luke Stainbridge, for I am now you. Now, do you want to go to the madhouse? You should have remained dead. I will give you an hour's start before sending my men.'

The man's confidence and arrogance seemed to wrong-foot the prisoner. 'Dead? Lost, you mean. Where is my cousin, Archibald?' he demanded.

'Behind the church, where he belongs.' The other smiled.

'No!' The stranger stepped back slightly, obviously realising that his cousin was dead and buried. This gave the gentleman an opportunity which he took without hesitation. He leapt from the bed and pulled repeatedly on the servants' bell.

Florence saw the poor man freeze, like a rabbit when it is caught in the hunter's sights.

'Sir,' she shouted into the room. He turned and looked at her as she stepped into the open doorway, 'They're coming!' Florence could hear shouts coming from below them, moving nearer as they left the servants' quarters and crossed the hallway.

'Who is that?' the gentleman asked, as he ran towards the door, but the captive sprang into action. Placing one foot on a chaise longue, he leapt in front of the other, planting a balled fist in the gentleman's cheek. The man fell, spread-eagled over the chaise longue.

'You and I are not finished. Sleep well if you can, because I will return to claim my birthright. Your days here are numbered!'

He ran through the open doorway and looked at Florence.

'Who are you?' he asked, but there was no time for her to explain. The two men were running up the lower flight of stairs. Florence felt the man's hand as he grabbed hold of hers firmly and ran with her to the end of the corridor

26

to the window, which she saw overlooked the grounds to the side of the building.

The gentleman had stumbled to his doorway. He leaned out holding onto the door frame. 'Get them!' he screamed at his men.

Florence was lifted bodily by the stranger; he unlatched the window and flung it open.

'Please don't! It's too far to jump!' she squealed. 'I'll break me neck!'

'No, it isn't,' he replied, swinging her feet over the sill. 'Trust me.'

Florence wondered why she should trust a stranger who was supposed to be destined for the madhouse — and if he were really mad. She clung to his body with both her arms wrapped around his neck.

Without time to question him further, she squealed as she was put down upon a lower roof, which she could only guess was the top of the servants' wing. It sloped, but she scrambled along it to the side, as did her fellow escapee, until she reached the end where a rickety metal staircase ran down to the grounds by the yard.

Without time to think of the danger or the height she clung to the ladder as it gave slightly, moving away from its brackets. This hastened her steps. Once her feet touched the earth, the stranger again took her by the hand and led her into the stables. He opened the stalls one by one as he entered, letting five horses loose in turn, slapping their rumps, sending them out in a panic across the stable yard to the open grass beyond the drive.

The male servants had started running across the cobbled stones. One had followed along the roof, the older had returned via the kitchens, but they both had to run for the safety of the wall as the animals were loose and running frantically. Finally, they reached the last stall. He lifted Florence high, setting her astride the animal. Quickly grabbing the bridle from the hook on the wall, he expertly slipped it over the animal's head and led it out of the stall and into the stable, the movement causing her to gasp. 'Hold on tightly,' he warned her.

He ran to the back of the stall, pulled up a piece of stone from the floor and retrieved a dusty old saddle bag, then swung his leg up over the back of the horse and kicked it on until it, too, galloped out across the yard. He whacked one of the servants with the back of the bag as the man tried to grab him to pull him off the horse.

They continued at speed across the cut lawns, not stopping even when a sharp noise echoed past Florence's ear. 'What was that?' she asked, and shook her head as if a fly had bothered her.

'They're shooting at us. Don't worry!' he spoke calmly, as they crossed the open country, bareback, with Florence hanging on for dear life, grateful that the stranger had a firm grip on her waist.

She glanced down. From above her knee to her boot she could see her exposed flesh. She felt an unusual sensation; this was freedom of a different sort to that she had imagined. Florence realised she was experiencing a freedom of action which placed her in a very vulnerable position.

Her plans had already gone terribly wrong. She was supposed to be hiding, lying low for a few months, before she went on her way to the city, and from there, to fulfil her plan for a better life.

So far, she had managed to get on the wrong side of a magistrate who may not be who he was claiming to be. Now she was being shot at, riding bareback and revealing her bare skin to a man accused of being mad, with the gentry in pursuit!

Florence could not think how, this time, she had managed to place herself so deeply in trouble with relatively little effort. Even Mrs Haggerty would not have expected her to achieve so much in such a short time.

Luke rode the horse to a sharp left turn which nearly had her slipping off the horse's back, if not for the strength in his arm around her waist holding her in place. They rode into a gap between the trees that covered the bank and followed a narrow track into its dark depth. They had to slow down while the horse picked its footing carefully on the downward sloping path.

'Who are you?' she asked.

'Funny, I was about to ask you the same thing,' he replied.

'My name is Florence Swan. And who are you?' she persisted.

'I am the man who rightfully owns that manor house. My name is Luke Stainbridge.' There was bitterness in his voice.

'So why are you mad? Or are you?' Florence tried to twist around slightly to see his face. He had the face and posture of the gentry, that she did not doubt, but he did not appear to be of dulled senses.

'I am more than mad, miss. I am furious. My name and my home have been taken over by an impostor and now, somehow, I have to prove it.'

She saw that he was tired. His eyes had lines in the corners and he had dark patches under his eyes — kind eyes, she thought distractedly, but still tired nevertheless.

'Tell me what you know about the man. How long has he been there? Does he have any of my original servants left? Tell me the truth of it and I shall see you are rewarded. I need your help. You might be able to help me without even realising it. I need to know when he came, with whom and what happened to poor Archibald. If he had a hand in his death, I shall see he pays tenfold. How long have you worked there?'

She swallowed. His eyes showed how desperate he was for her to help him. Florence wished she could help him by answering any one of his many questions but she had no answers for him, just more questions.

'I cannot help you,' she answered quietly.

'You need not fear him. I will protect you. I just need to know — '

'You don't understand, Mr Luke. I don't know the house at all. I had just arrived, I was hoping to find work but I never even got to introduce myself.'

He stopped the horse for a moment. 'You expect me to believe that you approached the manor, entered it without permission and just happened to be there in time to see me being locked up, and stayed long enough to witness my escape?'

'Yes, I do, but not completely. I only actually saw you breaking out of your prison,' she replied honestly.

He sighed. 'Miss Swan, I do not know if I should believe you. It sounds beyond credibility.'

'Then we both face the same problem, sir, for why should I believe a mad man — or a furious one, for that matter — who is adamant that a manor house belongs to him, yet the owner has a complete staff and is very sure of himself? He even looks a bit like you — but his nose is more angular and his eyes are harder.'

He did not answer immediately. 'You have a point.' He was thoughtful for a while and walked the horse along in silence. 'He does look a little like me, which is why, I suppose, allowing for the passing of years, he has been able to fool some people of his new identity. Surely, though, not all!'

Florence shrugged; it was all beyond her plans. Instead she found herself looking around and enjoying the smell of the foliage, the noise of birdsong and the feel of the horse beneath her — and the warmth and security of the arm that hugged her waist.

She wished the feeling of freedom, the abandonment of rules and constraints, would last a lifetime. It was so different from the stifling uniform existence of the mill school; she felt free, yet she was being hunted. Her world had changed completely. Florence could not understand why she was not gripped by fear. Instead, the danger had made her feel more alive. She breathed deeply, relishing the fresh, untainted air. Her moment of enjoyment ended abruptly as their path led them to a steep river bank.

'Now we're scuppered,' she said.

She felt him laugh behind her, his muscles contracting at her comments. 'You give in too easily, whoever you are. Hold tight.' He did not wait for a reply but flicked the reins and the horse found its way down the bank to the water. Their mount's back legs slipped a few inches on the wet mud and Florence gripped his arm.

'It's nothing to worry about. Let the horse find its way. Keep quiet. If they do not realise what I have done, we will put a few miles between us and them. Then we will be able to hide out for a while, which will give me time to think and for us to talk. I think you have some explaining to do.'

Florence could not reply as she found herself clinging to a horse whose legs were wading through the river's waters. Her own legs were as wet as the animal's.

'My boots will be ruined!' she exclaimed.

'They were ruined before you got on the horse, by the look of them.'

'They are my only pair!'

'Quiet, woman! I will find you new ones.'

'You are a thief?' she whispered her question, noting he called her a woman and not a girl.

'I am a gentleman, and my senses are telling me that you are trouble.'

She ignored his comment because she was in no position to argue with him. Florence could not swim and clung on for dear life, but her new-found 'friend' seemed not to notice or care.

He kept the bag he had retrieved from the stable high away from the water and watched either side at the banks until they finally came to a crossing point where he allowed the horse to find dry land again, and follow a track up to the road.

'Where are you taking me?' she asked, shivering.

'Somewhere safe,' he said, 'where we

can talk to each other properly.'

'And eat?' she asked hopefully.

'Perhaps.'

They heard movement up ahead of them along the road, so he walked the horse into the cover of the trees again. It skittered a little so she stroked its neck, which seemed to calm it. A small covered black cart went by. It had a lock upon the door at the back, and a man with a doctor's bag sat on the driver's seat. A liveried man, dressed in the same uniform as those in the hall, rode separately behind them.

'What was that?' Florence asked.

'My carriage, I believe.' He looked down at her kindly. 'But I shan't need it today, I think.'

He took off his jacket and placed it around her shoulders over the coat which she had found to be very thin, letting the cold air through its poor weave. Luke led the horse back onto the road where they galloped off in the opposite direction to the black asylum carriage.

3

Luke looked out of the barn door across the open field. This was not a good place to stay, he knew that; it was so obvious. However, they were limited for choices. He had to think quickly. The young woman was huddled in his coat in the discarded hay in the corner of the barn. Curled up like that she looked younger than he'd thought, and more vulnerable. He had not been able to pay her much attention at the time as he'd grappled with the situation at the manor.

His heart ached to see his home and possessions being used so by an impostor. It should be the easiest thing in the world to return home to one's own property. If he could return to London, he could prove who he was. That would take time; too much time. The man now knew he had survived, and returned, therefore he had two choices: firstly to hunt him and dispose of him, either from society, such as in an asylum, or permanently by murdering him. His appraisal of the man was that he would now seek to hunt him and have him killed. That way there was no possible future threat.

Luke had spoken in anger and haste and left the impostor with words of revenge ringing in his ear. Luke looked at the young woman, curled into a ball. What was he to do with her? Could he trust her? She might sell information back to the manor. Why on earth did she help him and involve herself in his nightmare? He leaned against the barn's old doorway, his head full of more questions than he had answers for. The horse was drying off slowly but needed to be rested. At least here it could feed — unlike them.

'We need to keep moving.' Florence's eyes opened, still sleepy. 'Tell me, where are you from? Perhaps we could return to your home. I could pay them for their silence, and then you would not have to go into service.'

He looked at her hopefully.

She had removed her boots, which he had filled with straw and left in what remained of the sun's heat outside in the open. She sat up, wriggling her dry toes, with his jacket wrapped tightly around her body. 'There is a difficulty with that idea, sir,' she said cautiously.

'I won't let them gain the wrong idea about why you have been travelling with me.' He blushed slightly, but hid his awkwardness with a grin.

'That's not the problem. You see, I don't have any folks of my own. I was orphaned young and have been in an establishment for some years where I have been given an education of sorts and learned to use my hands — lace making, weaving and domestic skills.' It was her turn to blush.

'How old are you?' he asked, as if appraising her for the first time.

'How old are *you*?' she asked defensively.

'Twenty eight, and you are?' He folded his arms and stared at her.

'Nearly twenty-one,' she answered, and tilted her nose upwards as if this would add extra maturity.

'Nearly?' He bent one knee and knelt in front of her, looking into her eyes. 'The honest-to-goodness truth, Florrie. We have enough problems without me being accused of absconding or kidnapping a young woman.'

There it was again — 'woman' — he had not called her a girl. He had also used a familiar name as opposed to her formal title. She loved the way he said it, but realised she was about to become a girl in his eyes.

'I was in a school owned by mill owners. They take young girls in and when they reach their twenty-first birthday they send them on to a big mill further west with promises of a good life. Only I know it isn't like that. I spoke to someone who has seen what the mill is like and knows what has happened to some of the girls — women who are sent there. It's not much better than slavery.'

'Benford's?' he asked.

'Yes, that's right — do you know of it?' She was surprised, yet if he were local it should not really surprise her because it had been running for nearly two decades. Benford Mill was a forward-thinking establishment — or so it presented itself to the outside world. They housed young girls from the age of eight; orphans, waifs or those whom their impoverished parents could not feed. In return the girls worked until they became women, when they were sent by open wagon to the large mills in the west.

They were told tales of a vast building, where they had a future, good food and a clean living. It was something they had to earn and work hard to aspire to. Lazy girls and those who were of weak-willed characters went elsewhere, but no one was sure where exactly that was. Most achieved the favour of the board and were sent on to their new life in the big mill.

It had become every girl's ambition to be sent west to where a more affluent life would greet them. Florence, however, was near the age of being sent away, but she had no intention of going.

'I know of it. I think you know little of the life, or existence, of a slave. I can return you, but I would not be able to explain this little escapade to them. They would merely send for the justice — and we know who is controlling that around here.' He sighed.

'Well, I may not know a lot about slavery, sir, as your gentry would of course, but I know what freedom is and that is not what I can expect at the mill. You cannot take me back there. I don't want to work in a mill.'

'There are worse things a girl could do.' He folded his arms.

Her heart sank when he had called her a girl. 'Perhaps, but I am not a girl. I don't wish to slave away in a mill, where rich men — gentry — will get even richer off my back — and I have no intention of earning a crust by lying on it!' Her voice had risen, as had her temper, and become louder. She had not meant to be so bold or crude, but wanted to set him straight. She may not have her majority and she may be a runaway who was in fairly desperate circumstances, but she had her pride and spirit intact; between them somehow, she would survive this ordeal, even though it had not been part of her original plan.

'You did not leave with their blessing,' he spoke calmly, rubbing his bottom lip thoughtfully with his thumb.

'No, I did not. You see I decided to be free, as you are, and I ran away.' She felt her cheeks flush.

'You boldly declare you have no intention of earning a crust upon your back and yet you ran away without any means and entered the scullery of a gentleman's house, unannounced. Do you seriously think you can survive in this world, thinking like that?' He shook his head.

Florence did not stop to think. Her pride was hurt. He had spoken to her

44

like a foolish child. 'Yes! I did and I can! I can look after myself. And it is I who helped you, and you who are in a bigger fix than me. You need not preach because — '

One minute she was spouting her defence at the man, a stranger whose path had somehow become entwined with her own, the next she was flat on her back lying upon the hay, with him straddled atop her, pinning her arms to the ground at either side of her head, his face only inches away from hers. Florence tried to bring her knee up to hit him sharply in his groin, but he shifted his weight so that his body pinned her down.

'Get off me or I will scream!' Her lips were silenced as his mouth pressed against hers in an unexpected, passionate kiss. It shocked her. His actions were so wrong, vulgar even, and yet, the rush of emotions triggered within her shocked her even more.

Fear mixed with indignation was sweeping through her body, causing strange sensations. The sudden rush of feelings was similar to those she had experienced when they had galloped across the field to escape — a spontaneous burst of uncontrolled excitement, wild and dangerous.

'Get off me!' she managed to repeat as he lifted his mouth from hers. She almost spat out the words as she regained her normal breathing. Desperation replaced all other emotions as a tear formed in the corner of her eye and slipped down her cheek. She had never felt so helpless.

He sat back on his haunches, quickly wiping the tear away with his finger. 'I hope that will not be the first of many tears shed from a naive heart, because, Florrie, you have been most unwise. I could have disgraced you here and now. I have no wish to, Miss Florence Swan. I am a soldier and, fortunately for you, I am a gentleman; the two do not always guarantee a lady's safety. However, I am an honourable man, unlike the one who has stolen my manor. I will not hurt you, I merely wanted you to realise how vulnerable you are. You have spirit, but that can be broken and crushed; the mill's school has not dented it but, believe me, one man — the wrong man — could. A young woman on her own cannot walk free in this land.'

She stood up, placing both hands on her hips. 'You do a trick like that to me again and I will hand you over to the magistrate myself!' She was shaking with indignation, as well as hunger.

'That you will not do, if for no other reason than you cannot do it. You are being hunted, as I am. You are a witness to what happened at the manor. You heard the man admit he was taking my identity away from me. So you, too, could end up locked away as a ranting lunatic in an asylum, or worse. So, I now have yet another problem to deal with, since he is also acting as the magistrate.'

Florence was still shaking. She was hungry and had been frightened by what he had done to her. His actions had shown her just how stupid and naive her plan had been.

He stood up; she did not recoil from his presence but looked into his eyes as he faced her. The words he had said had also struck her pride hard, because she knew they were the truth. She was in as much trouble as he; she had little enough to lose. Only one thing they could take from her was her precious newfound freedom — or her life. He placed an arm around her; she withdrew from his touch.

'I am truly sorry if I scared you, but I decided you need to know what men are capable of. You are no match for brute force. You needed to realise just how easy it would be for someone, like the blackguard in my home, to take advantage of you. You would have been safer in the mill. Your life would have been hard, but you would be guaranteed to have one, and eventually a family of your own.'

Florence allowed herself to curl into his warmth. In her heart she was grateful she had crossed his path and not that of the 'other' Luke Stainbridge, who was not an honourable man. But the last place she wanted to be at that moment was safe in a humdrum life, trapped in a mill where the noise deafened you and the air filled your lungs with fabric as much as air.

'Why have a family at all, sir, if their destiny is no more than to toil endlessly, nearly starve in winter, only to die of chills and diseases? I'd rather live alone and spare them and me the grief of it. If I followed your advice, I also might end up leaving a daughter alone in a mill school with no friends or family to call their own.'

She felt his hand pat her head gently, so stayed there against his warmth for a few moments, lost in the unusual feelings of safety and security found in his strong arms; realising just how contented they made her feel.

'Then stay with me and we shall work our way through this mess together,' he told her softly.

4

Mrs Haggerty had been taken to task over the whereabouts of the missing inmate, Miss Swan. She prickled with bruised pride as she strode away from the Beadle's office. There had been no word of the girl, Swan. None of the other girls had given even a hint of where Swan had gone, not even under the threat of a beating. Haggerty admitted to herself at least, that Swan had been clever and devious, which earned her at least a modicum of the woman's respect. No one had been Swan's confidant, therefore she had left no trail. The result was that Florence Swan had vanished from sight, not even the barge boy had seen her leave.

Mrs Haggerty was now being sent on a mission to take word to the sergeant of the local militia that they had a girl running loose in the countryside. The girl would not be fit for the mill now. She would be sent elsewhere; her reputation would be known, so the foolish girl had thrown an industrious life away for one which offered few prospects. Haggerty felt as though she was being forced to pay a penance; she had to explain how the girl had got away, as if she was to blame. She put on her coat and summoned the lad, Jonah, to fetch the small wagon.

'Be quick about it!' she snapped, fixing her hat securely upon her hair which was pinned high upon her head, making the lines around her eyes more severe.

'Yes, Mrs Haggerty,' the boy shouted, as he ran toward the old stable.

Haggerty stood waiting, silently cursing the girl. When she found her, she swore she would make her pay for the humiliation the wench had caused her. Never had one of her wards been as blatantly disobedient as the Swan lass had been. It was in her blood. Christopher Swan had been a blacksmith, and everyone knew what problems they could cause. They dared to learn their words and form opinions beyond their status.

Haggerty watched the wagon appear as she remembered the confident muscular figure of Christopher. So full of ideals, so full of words, and where had those ideals got him? Haggerty almost smiled as she remembered the scandal that blew up surrounding his case. New South Wales, that's where, and he and his high ideals were now a world away — a new world, that was. Her smile faded as the long-buried hurt returned.

★   ★   ★

'Who were your parents, Florrie?' Luke Stainbridge asked her, as she forced her feet back into her boots. They would rub if she had to walk any distance, so she was glad that her 'lunatic' had proved himself to also be a resourceful horse thief.

'Mr Christopher Swan and Millicent

Swan of Ebton. They were living in Gorebeck when . . . ' She tugged at her boot and winced as the damp leather pulled on her skin. The toe cap was still damp inside and the heel felt rough as she forced her foot inside, but at least they were mainly dry.

'You know who they were, that's good. So what happened to them? You said when; when what?' He leaned against the door of the barn watching her. 'What happened to them?'

She glared at him. Her pride had been hurt by his seemingly innocent, yet presumptive questions. 'You are surprised that the likes of me should know who my own parents are, and no doubt you will be shocked to know they were actually married. Your question is insulting, sir. Are you sure you really know who *you* are?' She snapped the question back at him and watched as an annoying smile spread across his lips.

'I am presumptive. I make no apology for it, because there are many illegitimate children who have no idea why they were left in such places. You are indeed fortunate, miss. Or, perhaps not so, because you know who you have lost — and that may cause you more pain. There is always more than one way to view a circumstance.' He regarded her thoughtfully. 'Christopher Swan, his name seems familiar.' He stroked the horse's neck. 'And let me assure you, miss, I know exactly who I am. Do not doubt that because it will be your salvation since, as I will be reinstated, I will reward you for your help as soon as I am able to. Now, though, we have to continue our journey. When we next stop, you can tell me what happened to them.'

'I might prefer not to.'

He seemed to ignore her comment, sweeping her up onto the horse's back. 'That is your choice,' he said. 'You have pride in abundance, Florrie, for one born so humbly. Bend your head as you leave the barn.' He walked her, on the horse, outside into the cool air of the evening. Florence stared at the beam above her as she rode underneath it with ample room.

'There is lots of room,' she said, with a puzzled expression on her face.

'Really? You hold your head so high that I wasn't sure there would be.' He smiled and winked at her.

She looked back at him; he was laughing at her as he climbed up behind her, but in no time they were crossing the open country again at speed. Again she hung on to him for dear life as he held her waist, and they travelled together, strangers yet inextricably joined in their quest.

He certainly seemed to know the country well enough, so she had no doubt of who he was, particularly after overhearing the conversation in the manor. It was only when they slowed to a halt as they approached a graveyard surrounding an old church, which was on the edge of a village near the coast, that he spoke to her again.

'Listen, Miss Swan, I need to enter this place in a clandestine manner. If I am found it will go badly for me, and terribly for you, but I have an idea of how I may find information to support my case.' He slipped off the horse, holding the reins in his hand.

'That is all well and good for you, sir, but how is that going to feed our empty bellies? The nag might be fed, but I am starving and cold.' She glanced back down at him and found he was looking most seriously at her.

'You are quite right. I am so driven by the injustice which has been done to me I quite forgot my own hunger. I am being very selfish, but I will find somewhere to leave you where you can be fed, and possibly find some work, and then I will continue to sort this mess out on my own. It will be safer that way.'

'Safer for whom?' She did not understand why she felt so desperate to stay with this strange man. It was as if fate had brought them together and Florence felt it would be wrong, or unsafe, for either of them to separate when they had so much to resolve. If he was telling her the truth, and there was no reason for her to doubt it, then he needed her as much as she needed him.

His actions in the barn may have been ungentlemanly and frightening in the moment, but he had achieved his goal. She no longer felt that same level of optimism and confidence which had taken her from the mill school to the manor house. Destiny had brought her and Luke together, where her adventure had begun. They were both being sought by his impostor, Luke II, as she had nicknamed him, who she believed to be as bent as a cat's hind leg, so she could not see how letting him walk away from her without knowing what happened to him next could be acceptable at all.

'We stay together; two heads are better than one. We need each other, Mr Luke, and I don't have anywhere to go. Because I became involved with helping you, my plans have been wrecked and now he, your other Luke, will want to silence me too. I am not keen to spend what should be the best years of my life in a lunatic asylum. You do not wish to, either. You have a home to reclaim, sir. So let's find food and then make another plan. I am good at that. Well, I had no problem making one, but then I had no way of knowing you would destroy the whole thing.' She shrugged.

'In your opinion, do you think I should apologise to you for destroying your ill-thought-out and doomed plan — or thank you for your help?'

'Perhaps both,' she said simply.

'What was your plan again? Oh, yes, I remember . . . you said it was to escape into a world which could so easily destroy you.' He cocked his head on one side. He was confident and annoying at the same time, because he had knowledge beyond her own, which in turn gave him wisdom and the ability to be right.

'No — to escape from life at a mill, find a placement that would earn me enough for a start in the city where I would find work in a ladies' dressmaker establishment and learn from the clientele. Then I would have my own business and work my way up to being a lady myself.'

She expected him to laugh at her, but he didn't.

'You have foresight and ambition beyond your years and position in life, I will admit that. However, that last statement you made shows that you would never have succeeded, Florrie, because, ladies simply do not work.'

She felt crestfallen. Money was the key to a better future, as she saw it, to a happier life and acceptance in society, but what did she know of the life of a lady? She only dreamed of one day being one.

'What is odd about you is that you have missed the most direct route for a pretty girl to find her way into any society.'

'And what is that?'

'To hook a gentleman and be his

mistress. It may not get you the position of a lady, but if you are pleasing enough and dedicated to the gentleman it would buy you the trappings of one. Instead you lay out this grand plan to work up every level in order to achieve it. Miss Swan, by then your looks would have left you, as would your energy — and it could never be, Florrie. Meeting me has saved you years of folly.'

'Why do you call me 'Florrie'? It is quite forward of you, isn't it?' She changed the subject, covering up, she hoped, the foolish whims of an inexperienced girl.

'Because I think it suits you. You may as well call me Luke, seeing as we have been stripped of rank and therefore protocol. It would appear that for the moment at least, we are in a situation where the rules of society do not apply. We are temporarily as outcasts.'

He was looking at the building beyond the church.

'We'll leave the horse tethered over

there in the shelter of those trees. Are you up for some honest thievery?' He smiled at her.

Florence noted that, when he relaxed his expression, he looked younger and more attractive. She could tell he was tired and shaken by what had happened to him. She wondered, as the person he should be, owner of a manor, whether he would even have spoken to her other than to snap out an order to a maidservant?

'Well we can't be in deeper trouble than we are at present, can we?' She smiled nervously back at him.

'Sadly, yes we could, but the vicarage normally has a well-stocked larder and I'm sure we will be able to ease our hunger at least.' He began to walk the horse over to the trees where it would be hidden from view.

'You can't really steal from a vicar!' she whispered. 'It wouldn't be right.'

'Giving to the poor, by default,' he explained, and shrugged dismissively.

'Have you ever stolen before?' she

asked, wondering if rich men stole for pleasure as poor men did for necessity.

'Miss, I have fought in wars. I have seen things not fit to explain or describe to your young ears. Just accept that, yes, I have had to steal to survive on occasion — as well as scavenge and kill. None of which I am proud to admit to and never would have by choice, but war brings men low.

'I nearly starved in a jail. I will not have my conscience pricked by needing to take the food from an overfed clergyman, which I intend to repay in time, when my home, land and what is left of my money and belongings are restored to me.

'You are hungry. Follow me, stay low and keep quiet and we shall eat. If you need to, run to the horse and head back for the barn. I will find you there if I encounter a problem.'

'If you encounter a problem, then I will stay and fight with you!' she said.

'No! You will clear out, because I will only be distracted if you stay. Please accept my orders for your own sake.' He patted her shoulder. 'Keep low, silent and follow me.'

He crouched down and made his way swiftly through the graveyard, skirting the wall of the church until they could stop and see the vicarage beyond. There was no sign of life or light in any of the windows.

'So far so good,' he said in a barely audible voice.

'You're good at this,' she commented. That surge of excitement was racing through her blood. She knew she should be scared and appalled at what they were about to do, but Florence guiltily had to admit to herself that she found the whole experience challenging and exhilarating.

Luke made her feel safe. She was not alone any more; she had a partner in crime. Like her father before her, she had never stolen a thing in her life, but she knew injustice when she saw it. Her father's experience of a corrupt law had taught her a strong moral code. This was the first time she had come anywhere near to breaking it, but it felt the right thing to do, so she would support Luke. She glanced down as her belly rumbled.

'Control that or we shall have the dogs on us.' He looked back at her.

'Dogs?' she snapped.

'It was a joke. We would have heard them if they were here. Are you ready for this? You can stay here and I will bring food out to you.'

'Two can carry more than one. Besides, I can be your lookout whilst you go and do the job.' She saw his eyes widen.

'Are you sure you have not done this before?' he asked.

'Positive, but I am good at planning. I told you that.'

'Yes, so you did, only . . . never mind. Come, and stay quiet. Any trouble and you must run and follow my instructions, or I will not know where to find you.' He set off.

Florence followed him thinking he

definitely would, because she had no intention of running anywhere without him.

* * *

Mrs Haggerty arrived at the militia's office on the edge of the Stainbridge Estate. It was really a converted stable block, which had seen grander days when the old hall had stood proudly next to it for nearly a hundred years. Unfortunately the building had burned down leaving the grand stable unscathed, to take pride of place as the largest and grandest of the remaining buildings upon the land. Luke's family had not the money to rebuild a hall in the same splendour, so a modern manor had been built over three years, nearer the river. The small office in the clock tower suited its current needs for administrative purposes. The horses were well looked after and had more space per head than the soldiers who rode them.

The soldiers were billeted in a building at the back of the stables, which had been a servants' hall. The men were expected to stay and not return to their homes as the war with Napoleon dragged on.

Their families had been allowed to share the accommodation so long as they never disrupted the duties or training of their menfolk. Any discord that erupted would result in them all being sent away, so they overflowed into the roof space above, living in an enforced harmony where the men had instilled their own law to make sure that peace ensued and disputes were quickly and harshly dealt with.

The women and children were allowed to leave by the back stairs of the building when necessary, and follow a track to the local town, but they were never to be seen on the square, which was surrounded on three sides by the stable buildings. The clock tower was above the archway to the stables.

So long as the families stayed out of

the way and no squabbles ensued, the military life carried on undisturbed, run by an ex-soldier, who was once an officer in the Peninsular Wars, called Brent. He had lost hair, his once athletic figure and most of his ideals. It was into the tiny clock tower office of Captain Josephus Brent that Mrs Haggerty was shown by a soldier.

'My dear lady, what can I do for you?' he enquired, as he gestured to the wooden chair opposite his desk. It was quite a rickety piece of furniture which had been saved from the original hall. Well made but, like the man, it had perhaps seen the best of its days go by. It was also made of a hard wood, making it as unyielding as the soldier could be, Mrs Haggerty thought.

The walls were crammed with ledgers, rolled-up maps and all manner of objects from sextants to old knives. In the corner was a trunk above which a fine sword had pride of place, hanging on what area of spare stone wall there was free to display anything. Behind him a small narrow window slit in the stone wall let in the only daylight. Three lamps lit the rest of the room. They flickered as Mrs Haggerty sat down, making the atmosphere incongruously close and cosy.

Haggerty liked the man's style, even if his room lacked her preferred standard of neatness. His uniform was clean, pressed and looked well enough on him despite his paunch. He was, she thought, a man who enjoyed his position in life as well as his food. She smiled coyly at him.

'Sir, it is a very delicate matter I have come to you to speak about. It requires haste and delicacy, as a girl — no, I should say a young woman — is lost and needs to be found. I am from Benford's Mill School and the young lady was one of my students.' She seated herself delicately upon the chair.

He propped himself on the edge of the desk in front of her, tilting his head as he listened attentively. 'Miss, you have my undivided attention.'

'Mrs Haggerty,' she corrected quickly, noticing a slight look of disappointment in his eyes. 'I was widowed young, sir. My husband was in the infantry and fell in '01.' She looked down for a second, partly to give the impression of a grieving lonely woman, but mainly to hide the look of glee the memory of his untimely death had brought. He had not been a kindly man, and she had been pleased when he was enlisted and was sent many miles away. His death had merely freed her from a life that would have been littered with beatings, as he drank with enthusiasm.

'You have my utmost sympathy and empathy, as I too was widowed not a year since. My poor wife was not of a hearty disposition and unfortunately succumbed to an ague, which ultimately took her away from me. Life can be so cruel. However, I digress, Mrs Haggerty. When and where did this woman go missing from? We must save her if we can, but her reputation, you will understand, may be already beyond repair.' He leaned forward slightly.

Haggerty sat, as her mother had taught her, with her back straight, shoulders relaxed and looked straight into the gentleman's eyes. She explained how she ran the school, how her duties kept her very busy and how her trust had been broken. Like many in the area, the school was a place he had heard of, or passed, even. It was as if he hung on her every word. She even felt a faint flush of colour on her cheeks. At the school she was summoned and dismissed as if she had no face, personality or life of her own to consider. This outing was rare, meant to humiliate her for her failings — a girl had slipped away under her watch — but in fact it was turning out to be an adventure in itself.

'She disappeared?' he said, folding his arms.

'Ran away . . . I fear she had — has — a spirit which was unbecoming to a young lady. I have tried to quell her hunger, but she is a wild child who yearns for something more from life than her position will give her. I fear I have failed her; I should have been a firmer taskmaster and broken that spirit before it brought her low — which I fear it may well have done so now.

'Florence has been given to flights of fancy, driven no doubt by a craving for adventure, fuelled by a novel called The Monk, which had been smuggled into the girls' dormitory. It was of a Gothic persuasion and definitely had nothing wholesome to do with the religious inference of the title. I fear they are in fashion, and try as we might, these wicked stories entice young ladies, who should not know of such passions, to have heightened feelings and inevitably to think sinful thoughts, even so far as to risk their reputations and destroy their lives. It is evil, sir.

'Please can you search for her? If you find her before her absence is widely known, then the scandal at least could be controlled or deflated.' She looked at him, appealing for his help, quite pleased with herself for thinking up

71

such a story, as the copy had been discovered when the school had been searched for clues on the instruction of the Beadle. She would use it now to get back at Swan. Haggerty had seen his eyes almost glisten as she spoke of the flames of sin being fanned in a young girl's mind. She had his measure; he was a lonely man.

'What is the wench's name and does she have family hereabouts?' he asked intently.

'Florence Swan, her mother is dead and her father . . . '

'Is serving a sentence in the penal colonies in New South Wales, if I am not mistaken. By God, if it has not been proven time and time over that rot does run through bad blood, I should be fair surprised to find a good man born of a bad one's seed! He's a thief and she is now a fallen wench!' He looked at her earnestly. 'I apologise for my graphic language, ma'am. I am more used to the acquaintance of soldiers and should have not offended such delicate ears.'

Haggerty let out a discreet gasp and covered her lips with her gloved fingers. 'There is no need, for I am surrounded all day by the children of paupers and am ashamed to say one hears more choice expressions than my parents would have cared to know. You have expressed, graphically, what I have thought, but did not wish to utter.'

He quickly placed his hands on her shoulders and looked directly into her eyes. 'Do not alarm yourself, ma'am. I can be the soul of discretion when needs be. I will find this young Jezebel and see she is returned to your establishment before she can defile the good name of the school or your good reputation. You leave it to Josephus. I will order tea and we shall look at a map. A young lass on foot, with little knowledge of the world beyond a corrupted text, cannot get far. I am surprised she could even read.'

'Her father was an educated man, and of his profession a forward thinker, or rebel. He taught the girl her letters and discussed issues with her that a woman, let alone a young child, need not bother their heads with. The result is a wilful girl who does not know her place, who wastes her time being fanciful about things she hardly understands.

'Look where it has led her, to a path toward her own ruin. She will never find a suitable man. I doubt the mill owners will want her in their establishment now because she could spark unrest and trouble with her wild talk and notions. No; once she is restored to us, she will be punished and Mr Carrie will escort her to the city where she will work in one of the factories.'

He walked over to the door, opened it, and bellowed his order for a tray to be brought forthwith. She admired his authority, had felt her heart beat a little faster as he held her within his grasp and tried to compose herself.

He stepped back into the small room. 'Tell me, does Mr Carrie take many girls to this city factory?' he asked, curiously.

'Only the stupid or the headstrong are taken. Most of our young women work hard to learn and are found decent positions at the mill — running teams or marrying the better workers. It is only the idle and ungifted who are taken to the city. Their chances of attaining anything other than a living wage for themselves are very poor.' She shrugged, she had not questioned this further because Mr Carrie was a kindly man and he insisted on finding a safe place for those less able himself. Haggerty had just been glad to see the back of any she considered stupid or wilful. It was not her place to question his decisions and she did not want to know anything different to what she had been told.

He seemed to accept this explanation and smiled at her in that friendly manner that made his dark eyes shine at her.

'Now, my dear, let us consult the map.' He turned to a shelf and brought down a roll of parchment from where it was balanced; he unrolled it whilst standing next to her. It slipped from his fingers and sprang back. Both of them reached for its edge to replace it and their arms touched, eyes stared into each other's as they leaned forwards. She smelt tobacco on his breath and breathed in slowly. She smiled as his cheek was almost touching hers and sat back. He reached for a paperweight, an ink bottle and a book to anchor it before glancing back at her.

'Now, I must decide upon the best place for my men to start the search. Then, once the soldiers are on their way, I shall see you safely back to the school.' He looked at her, as if seeking her approval.

Haggerty's heart beat a little faster. She had not felt this way in a man's presence for nearly a decade, and had never expected to feel that heady rush of excitement again. Yet Josephus appeared to touch her inner soul, and she knew not how.

'Thank you, sir,' she murmured. 'I

am so sorry to have to decline your offer as you have been so kind. I have a wagon outside and a boy waiting.' She genuinely looked saddened. To travel with such a man and in a carriage . . . oh, it was like one of the novellas she read! If only he would whisk her away from the school and make her his own . . .

She stroked the fabric of her skirt and sat neatly with one hand cupped inside the other. She had to regain control of her inner thoughts. If her composure gave away any hint of inclination as to how she was feeling, her reputation would also lie in tatters. She had no wish to find out for herself if the factory in the city truly existed.

'Merely doing my duty, ma'am. I shall be glad of the opportunity to share a carriage with you and see you safely back. I will tell the boy to return forthwith. No use leaving him to become no more than idle hands. Besides, a lady like yourself should not travel in an open wagon — and I will also be able to speak to the Beadle and find out more about this lass.'

Mrs Haggerty smiled politely at him, but it was inside her that the smile grew ever broader, and for the first time in a very long time she felt what could only be described as true happiness.

5

Luke skirted around the building with Florrie close behind him. She had scooped her skirt up and had it bunched around her knees as she crouched next to him. He glanced back to say something to her but was momentarily distracted by her appearance. Her hair had lost a pin in the barn when he had pushed her down. The following ride had loosened her hair, which now hung over her shoulder, its natural fairness accentuated by the moon's glow, and her calves also reflected the lunar light.

He had not realised how attractive she was until he had been so close to her in the barn. His mind was filled with an underlying rage, and a need to re-establish his life as it had been, happy and free before he had gone into the army to fight for his country. It had sounded a noble ideal and, as a youth who was set to inherit the manor and whatever lands his father still owned, he had had many ideals.

Gradually over six long years they had been eroded. He had been glad to be free and had decided that, after some time with Archie in the countryside, he might just be able to think once more as he had then, with optimism rather than cynicism. He realised that, with Archibald now gone, that optimism was forever threatened. He had looked at the stones around him and thought it was as if the graveyard was almost mocking his grief, serving only to accentuate the realisation that nothing could be as it was again.

Now, here in this lonely place, so close to him was a vision of loveliness, with a will of iron but the knowledge of a fool regarding worldly issues. How fate played with his mind. At a time when he should feel nothing but empty bitterness, this fresh-faced woman was filled with her own ambition, determination and will; naive to those who could so easily crush her spirit.

The years of wanting and longing in a prison cell had been almost unbearable, but he had kept his sanity planning his return home, deciding that once he had spent a few months with Archibald he would enter into a quest to find himself a suitable partner for life; if not a love-match then one of comfort and convenience.

Looking at her, he was aware that his feelings were moved. She was pretty, innocent and not world-weary as he now was. What a companion she would make, despite her lack of breeding. Here he was with his home out of his reach, next to this warm creature with those large trusting eyes, like deep pools, looking to him for her next instruction. How would he keep her safe if they were caught?

He closed his eyes for a moment to refocus his thoughts. He was hungry and tired and that, on top of his shock and despair, was making him irrational and emotional.

'Are you all right, Luke?' she whispered in his ear, so close to him so that she would not wake the dead, for, other than the grave stones marking the final resting place of those who had left this world already, there was little sign of any other life.

He felt the warmth of her breath upon his skin and moved a little away from her. He was definitely being distracted; he must find them food and retrieve his normal senses and control, his common sense.

'Come, in silence!' he mouthed back at her.

She followed, looking slightly crestfallen and he led them to the back window of the vicarage where the scullery was situated. He did not look back at her again but focused on his present mission. He had to think of her as one of his men. He almost laughed, mocking his own sanity, for how could he ever view Florence Swan as anything other than a lovely young woman in her prime?

*   *   *

The air was cool by the time Mrs Haggerty and the Captain made their way down the narrow stairs from his office in the bell tower towards the yard, where a small coach was just stopping a few paces from the door, pulled by two fine horses. A man in fine uniform, the ostler, jumped down to the ground and approached the door, which he opened, and carefully unfolded a step for her to use to climb inside the carriage. It was a well worn and quite pokey vehicle which had the odour of leather polish mingled with stale smoke from, she guessed, the Captain's pipe, but it was a carriage and that was all Mrs Haggerty cared about.

When the Captain entered, he leaned over her as he positioned his rump on the opposite seat. Their eyes looked into each other's as if they were both trying to read the other's thoughts. It was for Mrs Haggerty an intimate moment, for she was not used to people being so close to her. She had never cuddled or preened over any of the children who had come into her charge. To allow closeness was to give away one's feelings, and she knew to her cost when one gave away one's emotions, others took them and left a gap that was difficult to fill.

He sat opposite her, his knees resting against hers, overlapping her space. Across the square, soldiers were leaving in a formation of two lines. A mounted section rode out ahead of them in a single line whilst the others followed on foot.

'You trust Josephus, Mrs Haggerty, I will find Swan for you and I promise she will be dealt with in a discreet and suitable manner. Now we have a little time to pass, so tell me about the dignified and immaculate Mrs Haggerty — I am all ears.' He placed one hand upon the seat at either side of him as the coach pulled away and, in his now familiar manner, smiled warmly at her.

She could feel herself blushing. This,

she mused, was quite ridiculous, even on her marriage night she had not blushed so much, but then that was because Henry had got drunk and crashed onto the bed, sleeping heavily for hours. The much-awaited nuptials took place in a half-hearted manner when he roused at dawn.

Her first beating followed the next day when she had complained bitterly about his behaviour. He had left for the continent within the month, never to return. From that day to this she had not allowed her heart to be touched again, until she had met the rather strange and alluring man opposite.

He wanted to know her, she sensed it, but there were things he would never know about her. 'What would you wish me to tell you?' she asked, warming to the game he played. He would not control her, even if he had touched her heart, her head had seen too much to give in to a whim of fate.

'Your name . . . I'm sure your given name would be more than suitable for one with such a caring nature and wholesome eyes.' He stared into hers.

She smiled, enjoying his outrageous flirting. 'Amelia Grace,' she replied.

He chuckled. 'And I have no doubt that you are educated, Amelia, for you have a refined air about you. It is my guess that you have been born of gentle stock. What a shame your husband had not left you in an independent position of means. How thoughtless he was — excuse me if my words insult your memory of him. I merely speak as a man who would want better for my widow, should I have left her when she was yet so young, for you must surely have been a child bride.'

'You flatter me greatly. I am not offended, but I married for love, and therefore brought my downfall in circumstance upon myself. I was lucky to be given a position of such responsibility at the mill school. My father was a clergyman, quite a mature man when I was born, and my mother a mere surgeon's daughter, but I thank you for

86

your flattery nonetheless.' She glanced out of the window.

He placed a hand upon her knee, which snapped her head back sharply so that she glared at his face, as he had leaned over toward her. The vehicle rocked as it traversed the ruts upon the road.

'You are forward, sir!' she said abruptly.

'Yes, I am and I make no apology, for I am of an age that I have little time to become acquainted with you and I am an old fool, but Mrs Amelia Haggerty, I would express my desire to know you much better. If you would be my mistress I would pay you well. I am a man of means and I have a position in the county.'

He leaned closer, laughing when she slapped his face. He sat back and folded his arms across his chest. 'Your answer is for the time being a resounding 'No' then, I presume — please do not try to slap me again, once was perhaps justified — no more.'

'You presume rightly, sir. If we were nearer to the town I would walk there on foot. How dare you?'

'Because you and I would enjoy life together . . . very much so. You know it, sweet Amelia, and so do I. That lack-lustre look that glazed your eyes when you entered my office has vanished, and in its place there is a spark. Oh, how I could make it burn so brightly.'

'You flatter yourself, sir.' She stared at him, his smile so relaxed it was as if he cared not for her protestations and would disbelieve them anyway.

'So you are not to be a mistress; I am glad. If you would be so easily swayed, then I would not stay with you long. So, I will make you another suggestion, a more agreeable proposition, I hope. Mrs Amelia Haggerty, allow me to court you for three months. If at the end of the three months you are not appalled by my blunt manner or my frank ways, then I will ask you to wed me and return with me to my home in

Suffolk. There we can both sparkle to our hearts' content. I, with your companionship and care, and you as the lady of my house and my legal wife with all that entails.'

'You would propose to me on such little acquaintance?' Haggerty was genuinely shocked.

'I am propositioning you. Three months and, if we have found a mutual ground of friendship, we will wed and you shall return to my home as my wife. Do we have an accord?'

She watched him. His manner suggested he was in earnest, but it seemed such an outlandish thing to happen to her. 'I need time to think this through; my reputation . . . '

'You have until this carriage arrives at the school. It will be the beginning of the most entertaining three months of your life, or a missed opportunity, dear Amelia. How many of those come your way and how many can you afford to let pass by?' He watched her but she did not respond. 'But I shall not repeat either offer again and, if I am rejected out of hand, the next time we meet will be as total strangers.'

'But we are now,' she replied.

'That can easily change,' he answered.

Haggerty stared at his hand but did not slap him this time. The coach approached the town. 'Very well, you can assume we will court for three months,' she whispered as the coach stopped and the soldier unrolled the step for her to dismount.

The Captain nodded. 'Excellent!' he said, and sat there for a moment before coming out.

So the novel had been her story, after all.

He smiled. He missed not having a woman around and this one looked fit, strong and had the potential to truly sparkle. He would enjoy breathing life back into her bones. He sighed before alighting. Now to find the hapless lass who had done a runner. *Silly girl*, he thought.

6

Florence felt ashamed as Luke had cast her a long dark look, and then had turned away from her, with what she could only surmise were feelings of disgust. She covered her legs and let her skirt fall onto the ground. He was used to being in the company of real ladies and she behaved like an uneducated scallywag, a runaway with no sense of propriety and — he no doubt believed — few morals. She was a common wench and, as such, behaved accordingly. It was a wonder he had not continued in his boorish behaviour; he said it was a warning to her of what men were capable of, but perhaps it was what he pictured her becoming.

He reached up to a narrow window. He felt the edges of the ledge, then slipped his fingers against the lower pane and gently pushed it. It had not been latched properly and slowly it slipped open. Then, he raised himself up to tiptoe, eased his weight forward till his shoulders were wedged between the frames and peered inside. Finally, he returned to his initial footing and looked down at her.

'I need you to slide inside here, lower yourself down carefully onto the floor and open the kitchen door so that I can enter. This window is too narrow for me to squeeze through.' He pointed to a larger window which was in front of a hardy stone sink nearer the door which was fastened securely. 'Do you think you can do that? It might help if you slipped off your coat; then the material will not catch on the latch as you slide down inside.'

She stared at him. 'I will enter the building, but I will not undress.'

'Then take extra care not to get hooked up on the latch. There is a sharp drop at the other side; you need to be careful. If you end up dangling there I will not be able to do much to help you, will I?'

'Lift me up so that I can see,' she whispered.

With his hands placed firmly around her waist he lifted her high enough for her to slip her arms and torso through the open widow. She felt his hands move from her waist, one against her lower back, the other supporting her rump. It was the most undignified position she had ever experienced. She was scared, yet it was all so exciting and different.

She wondered what he was thinking or if his mind was firmly upon wreaking revenge upon Luke II. She concentrated on the task in hand. Inside was the kitchen, with its hard stone floor below her, upon which was a higgledy-piggledy assortment of dolly tubs, pails, dustpans and a couple of wooden chairs next to a well-worn table. Overhead, linen drying racks were suspended from the ceiling and a fire and small range took pride of place in the end wall, next to the copper for laundry. Beneath her, some four feet lower down, was the unyielding floor. She gestured with her hand for him to pull her back down.

'I know I shall regret this. I will have to go in feet first and facing the wall or I will have nothing to hold as I slide down.' She unhooked the front of her coat and, standing with only her thin wool dress and her even thinner under garments covering her already cold body, she handed it to him. Now he could see her in her drab uniform. At least the coat looked as if it had once belonged to someone with a modicum of style. 'You pass that through to me as soon as I am in. Mind those hands of yours, and remember this is your idea and not mine!'

'Very well, but you must be careful. Open the door as soon as you can. If they hear you, I will still be outside. I won't leave you alone, but I will not be able to get to you without breaking down the door.'

'Just let's just get in before the vicar opens the door himself and invites us both in for tea. If I get caught, you must run to the horse, take it to the barn and when I am free I shall find you there.' She winked at him as she returned his own orders to her.

'Very witty . . . now are you ready?'

'Quick, before I freeze to death,' she whispered. He held her waist and swung her up so that she could slip her legs through the window, turning once when she was halfway through the small space. He changed his grip as her arms encircled his neck; her cheek was resting next to his, his breath caressed her skin. 'Gently push me up.'

He did so, very gently and, as she slid down the inside she transferred her grip to hold the window sill. It was a strange feeling being suspended from a window in a stranger's home, but she took a step in faith and allowed herself to drop to the floor below.

The room was lacking life and atmosphere and it was dark. Both made her feel oddly comforted by the feeling of isolation that it gave, yet there was a feeling of security at being within a building again. Being outside, having nowhere to go, had felt strange to her. The school had been her home, and prison, for nearly ten years. She hated it, yet it was real and tangible, and there was a comfort in a way of knowing what would happen each day. Now she had no idea where she would be in the next few moments, let alone tomorrow — which was different, threatening and yet irresistibly exciting.

However Florence had no wish to meet anyone here. She tiptoed over to the door. Her body felt as if it was losing its heat. The old coat had kept her moderately warm, but in here she was cold. The fire had long since been extinguished and there was no sign of cooking upon the hearth. The door was bolted in three places. She carefully pushed each iron bolt in turn and then turned the handle. Luke was in, in a second and wrapped her coat around her shoulders as soon as he had left the door slightly ajar. He had not tossed it through the window but kept it close to him.

'Why not close it?' she said quietly. 'If someone out there sees the door has been left slightly open, it will look odd.'

'It pays to leave an escape route open.' He went straight to the larder where the food would be stored. She followed behind him, her stomach growling as she thought about the food they were about to steal. Children had been hanged for less — her own father wrongly accused and transported for the finding of property that was not his.

He glanced down at her and she shrugged her shoulders back at him. 'Take some cheese, bread, and that ham.' He picked up a bottle of wine from the rack under the shelf and scooped up a tray of biscuits into a piece of muslin that was obviously kept for straining or steaming. 'That's enough,' he announced.

Florence used another piece of cloth to pour in some loose tea from a jar and then knotted the top.

'Are you going to pack a kettle also?' he asked.

'You never know when the opportunity to use one will occur.'

He shook his head and gestured that they should leave. This time the window and back door were closed properly. He led them straight over to the church and forced open the door by the back of the building. It was old and solid, but the single bolt that should have been set across the lock had not been slipped through.

'They don't expect people to break in here, do they?' she commented as they made their way through the vestry to the altar.

'Perhaps not. I hope no one feels the need to be here tonight. Lay the food on the pew there and we shall eat, then I shall see if the records tell me more about poor Archibald's death.' He found a candle and lit it, striking a spark twice before it took hold.

She busied herself proportioning the rations and tasting the food as she did

— 'lest it be off,' was her justification.

'It's good, Luke. Here sit still and eat. It will do you good. No one can think straight on an empty stomach. Then you can tell me why you think your Mr Archibald is dead.' She moved to sit on the other side of the food, leaving him room at the end of the pew. He ate with relish, as did Florence.

'Vicars eat well, don't they?' she commented.

He looked at her for a moment, before speaking. 'Not as well as the gentry, but a deal better than prison rations.'

'So who said he was dead? How did it happen?' she asked.

'The impostor said he was 'behind the church where he belongs'. That can only mean one thing.' He bit into a piece of ham as if he were considering ripping off Luke II's head.

'What?' She saw him stop mid-bite as he stared at her as if she was being deliberately dense.

'That he is buried in the graveyard,

behind the church — dead!' He coloured, obviously upset at the thought and frustrated by her lack of understanding of something so apparent.

'That isn't what he said, though, is it?' She picked up a piece of bread, before sipping from the bottle of wine which he had opened, forcing the cork down with his knife. She was surprised when he took hold of her wrist, gently, but preventing her from lifting the bread to her mouth.

'This is no time to play with words or my senses. Say what you mean!' His voice rose slightly and both became aware of this as they looked around into the shadowy corners of the building. When nothing stirred, she pulled her wrist from his grip and handed him the bottle of wine.

'Here, you hold that if you need a firm grip on something and leave me alone. I'm not playing with you at all; it's just that he didn't say the man was dead, just that he was behind the church. Well, that doesn't mean he is. If

you look at this one, what's behind it?'
She pushed the bread into her mouth
followed by some ham and stared at the
man opposite's face. He looked struck
dumb.

'The vicarage is behind the church
— this church, anyway. The manor only
has a small chapel, and that is built
against the wall of the herb garden. The
family graves are all before or to the
side of it.'

He drank from the bottle, and then
stared at the label. 'It is a fine wine, a
good vintage from the cellar, I would
bet. Archie liked his fine wines . . . ' His
face broke into a broad smile, he bent
forward and kissed her lips. It was a
glancing gesture at first which lingered
when he seated himself once more
leaning over their half eaten rations.

She pulled away, as much to catch
her breath as to protest . . . No,
'protest' was not the right word.

Luke stood up as if he was unaware
of any impropriety — but then, she
mused, why should he be? She was but

a simple, common wench and he was a gentleman.

'Come, Miss Swan, leave these things, I have been a fool. We shall announce ourselves at the vicarage and all will be well in our world again.' He took hold of her hand and led her towards the door.

Florence went willingly enough, but her heart felt heavy. Her world would never be so straightforward again. She had left a school with ideas of working her way up in life.

Then she had met a gentleman, who had shown her dreams for what they were — futile; he had had his land stolen from him, and had in turn had shown himself to be a thief — of a horse, of food, and of a young and lost woman's naive heart.

7

The captain walked into Mr Carrie's office shortly after Amelia Haggerty. He deliberately left a few paces between them so that it was not instantly apparent to Mr Carrie that he was there. As he suspected, her reception was not going to be warm.

'Haggerty! What is the meaning of this? We have been waiting all afternoon for word of what has happened to Swan or if you had reported her absence to the militia, then the boy comes back alone with you still at large. We wondered if you, too, had got it into your head to leave us!' The man's voice boomed around the room.

'Mr Carrie, sir, I have been with Captain Brent reporting the absence of Miss Swan as you instructed and I am pleased to say . . . '

Her voice was quieter than it had

been when the captain had spoken to her. It was the tremulous voice of an intimidated woman. Yet the captain had seen a much more confident side to her when she had been relaxed with him in his office.

'And has he found her or did you pass a pleasant afternoon discussing how Napoleon fares?' the man said sarcastically.

'I am afraid we did not have time to discuss such fascinating subjects,' Captain Brent interrupted. 'However, this fine lady has explained in detail how the girl is adrift and threatens the very name of your good school by the way in which she has so selfishly acted upon a fancy. My men are currently out searching and will report back to me at the barracks within the hour. Should you wish to add any more details about the girl then I am here, since I have escorted Mrs Haggerty safely back, as I was surprised she was made to travel in an open wagon.'

He entered the room in his immaculate

uniform and squared up to Carrie who was seated behind his desk, his hands placed firmly down on its top. His eyes widened as the captain appeared and he had the decency, from anger or embarrassment, to flush slightly at that comment.

'Haggerty's gross incompetence has lost us a young woman who our charitable institution had been preening in readiness for a position at the main mill!' The man was standing up behind his desk. He was tall, greying and imposing with dominant eyes that were almost as grey as his hair.

'I hardly think that she could have watched the girl continuously. Had this particular young woman a history of misbehaviour or of attempting escape?' he asked, watching the other man's stare intensify.

'No, not at all, but she was known to be a headstrong wench who offered more of a challenge,' he admitted.

'Really, then I am surprised that she was destined to work in the main mill where the well-behaved ladies are known to be sent. Surely if she was so spirited then you would have taken her to the other 'factory'?' He did not explain further. He watched the man's hesitation and knew what he suspected was true. This man found places for those less able girls.

Mr Carrie walked around the desk, standing before Amelia. 'Mrs Haggerty, it has been a most trying day, and it has not yet ended. Go and see to the other girls, they have been greatly upset by Swan's absence. I will see the captain out.'

Both men watched her leave the room. She had glanced thankfully, or hopefully, in the captain's direction before leaving; he had half-smiled which was the most he could do for now. His next mission was to get to the Swan girl before Carrie got his hands on her. He instinctively disliked the man.

'Sir — Captain — I have no idea what you infer, but some young women would be a danger to themselves and other workers in the mill, so they have to be found positions more suited to their natural gifts. That is not your concern here. Finding the runaway wench is and restoring her to the safety of the school should be your only concern and your goal.' He walked over to the door and held it open. 'Thank you for returning Mrs Haggerty safely to us. I see no need to detain you from your quest any further.'

The Captain's foot rose up so quickly that Carrie did not have time to stop him from slamming the door shut. 'Now, sir, I will speak to you. I will ask questions and if I am not happy with the answers given to me I will demand to see your records of where the last half dozen young wenches who have left this establishment are now working. This is supposed to be a place where innocent girls are educated and cared for. If I find proof that they have been abused, or you have used them to profit from them in a diabolical way, then your school will close!'

* ★ *

Mrs Haggerty could not eavesdrop any more, as the raised voices subsided, so she returned as she had been told to, to the dormitory where the girls were anxiously waiting for news of their spirited friend. She had hoped to see Josephus again in private, just for a few precious moments to arrange how they were to 'court' — if he had truly meant what he had said to her in the coach — but it was not to be. He had business with Mr Carrie so, solemnly, she returned to her duties.

However the feelings he had stirred inside her would not subside; yet her book had been tossed into the school's fire as a lesson to them of what they did with such despicable novels. She had watched with regret, because she had savoured every word, hiding her inner feelings whilst trying to keep upon her face a look of utter disgust as she surveyed the bewildered and innocent girls. Now all she had to look forward to was a distant promise, or a drab and thankless existence.

★   ★   ★

Florence followed Luke back to the vicarage; he made straight for the front of the building. 'Luke, let's go in the back way again. If I am wrong this could be a dangerous situation for you. Or at least let me knock on the door and you stay back, out of sight. That way I am only a lass looking for help. If you recognise the man, then step forward. If you don't then, well, I'll think of something to say. Who will be looking for me on my own?'

He stopped and considered her suggestion for a fleeting moment and then took her to the kitchen door.

'He will not answer the door himself. He will have at the very least a maid. You would wake her or his housekeeper and then you would, if they let you, be taken inside. So your plan would fail at the very onset. We will find our way to his room and then take it from there — but if you are wrong, our situation has just become a great deal more complex.'

She smiled at him, hoping to reassure him that she would not be wrong, trying to look confident. He raised one eyebrow and then opened the kitchen door letting her slip inside behind him, and leaving it slightly ajar.

They walked as quietly as they could from the kitchen along a short corridor which had a small room on one side where a woman snored away happily, undisturbed by their intrusion. Florence realised she was holding her breath lest it made a sound and presumed this must be the vicar's housekeeper or cook. Whoever she was, she gave no sign of consciousness and slumbered on.

The room opposite housed the linen and dry stores. They followed the short corridor until they came to flight of dark wooden stairs built onto the building's wall. Ahead of them were two doors to the left and one to the right. The house's front door was straight ahead. Luke stopped a moment and waited, holding his finger to his lips in case she spoke. There was no sound to be heard other than the slumbering woman's breath behind them so they continued up the stairs as quietly and as light of foot as they could.

The building was not vast. It had four upstairs rooms that they could make out. Luke slowly opened the doors to the first two to find they were as ghost rooms, covered in dust sheets, smelling slightly cold and stale. Life had not visited them in the recent past.

The third door, however, opened on to a room richly decorated in fine brocades, the overwhelming colour, from the drapes to the hangings on the four-poster bed to the rugs, throws, and evening coat which hung upon a stand, was a rich deep red. The cords were gold, plants on the mantelpiece above the fire which still burned low in the grate offered a contrast of hanging green, but this boudoir smacked of luxury, comfort with a slightly tasteless style. 'Archibald,' Luke muttered as he let them in and closed the door behind him.

Florence tapped his arm and pointed to the door. 'Exit route,' she whispered, reminding him of what he had told her earlier.

'We won't need one now,' he said, as he approached the bed. 'I have found him, he is here.'

Florence felt uneasy. This was not right. There were no robes visible. The room looked bawdy, with no cross or bible displayed, or seemingly present. This was not the room of a vicar and if it were not, then who was in the room they had not yet entered?

This man was a guest here or had been given a home here — why? She thought this through as she saw Luke lean over the figure in the bed. He was about to touch the sleeping man and gently rouse him when Florence tiptoed over to him and gently pulled him backwards.

'What are you doing?' He gestured to the bed. 'This is Archie!' His voice was still low, but his desperation threatened to drive it higher. She placed her finger to his lips.

'He isn't the vicar,' she whispered, gesturing around the room. 'That man must be next door.'

'Well, it doesn't matter now. Once he wakes, we are saved. He is here, alive, he will not have forgotten me.' Luke's smile was broad.

'Well, if he believes the man in the manor is you, then he is not in his right senses and will think you are the impostor.' Her voice was barely audible. She saw the light of what she was saying dawn across his face. In his excitement he had been rash and forgotten to think it through. 'Yes, he is Archie, but look at him; he is flat out.' She pointed to a small bottle of a dark liquid, which was at the side of his bed on a salver.

Luke picked it up and removed the stopper, sniffing it. 'Laudanum! Some- one has drugged him.'

'Yes, and we need to leave quickly before we are discovered.' She took the small bottle from his hand and replaced it. Then she slipped her hand in his and tugged him back towards the door.

'We can't leave him, not like this.' His face was flushed again, anger showing with the frustration and concern he obviously felt for his cousin.

She stood before him, turned his face to look straight at her. 'We know where he is. They want to keep him here. We need to leave now and make a plan. We can do nothing for him, or us, if we are found here, can we?'

Her words seemed to drift through his befuddled mind and she saw realisation return to his eyes. He quickly kissed her lips, took hold of her hand and they left.

He was a wronged man, driven by his outrage and in a fairly desperate situation, but they had to be clever and out-manoeuvre Luke II before the net closed in on them. They needed to outwit those who had stolen his property, and to do this she had to remain free.

That, she thought, would be easy because there was not going to be any great fuss made of one lost girl. Not after the first day of looking, of that she was sure. Neither Mrs Haggerty nor Mr Carrie would want to admit that a slip of a lass had out-flummoxed them. Florence dared to hope she at least would be free to help Luke through his living nightmare, and the thought gave her hope that in time her life may yet turn out well.

* * *

They rode away from the vale, across the moor to a lonely cold place where a group of fishermen's huts nestled behind the sand dunes, beyond a strange marshy land where a salt industry had once thrived. In the distance the sea crashed onto the flat sandy beach between the mouth of the river Tees and the distant headland of Stangcliffe.

'What is this place?' Florence asked, as he lifted her down from the horse's back. The feel of his strong hands circling her waist seemed almost natural to her now. She had been lonely for years, never seeing the other girls as her friends, because they sought this new life at a mill and a husband to go with it, but she wanted to be free and to think for herself.

'A nest of fishermen's huts, where if I am lucky — bearing in mind it is not a word which I have had much connection with of late . . . ' he brushed a hair from her cheek with his gloved finger, before continuing, 'except for meeting the resourceful Miss Swan, that is — it should be the one place I can still find an old friend.'

He lifted from her hand the wrapped victuals that they had retrieved from the church before leaving, and tied the horse's reins to an anchor which was lying between the huts. Luke then knocked on one of the huts' green doors.

Florence stood close to Luke as the wind was blasting over the dunes and straight at them. It was, she decided, the most unwelcoming place they had been, and the fresh air she craved was a bit *too* fresh here.

'What is?' a gruff voice boomed out from behind the closed door.

'I is,' Luke answered, beaming as he answered in the style of what sounded like a cryptic password.

'You is?' the surprised voice replied, and then the door opened.

'Aye, I is, Obadiah, and you are the most beautiful sight I have seen since I arrived back here.'

Luke almost threw his arms around the older, bearded man, despite the wind blowing so hard that the man had to hang onto a rope holding his door from being blown off its hinges. The man stared at her from beneath his wool hat. His hair, grey and wiry, seemed to sprout from beneath it, framing his craggy, salt worn skin.

'Well I can see one more beautiful

face — more than mine is, for sure. You best come in, but, be warned, me parlour is not ready for a young lady to visit.' He winked at her in a friendly manner and let them step inside.

In the middle of this small hut, no more than five feet wide by nine feet in length she guessed, was a little stove which blew steam out of a tiny hole-cum-chimney in the roof. There was one old chair, fishing nets and tackle to the side of it. Empty bottles were stashed at one end, with tools and a pair of long boots and southwester. A pewter plate, knife and mug were on the floor next to a little three-legged stool near the stove.

'You best sit down here, next to the warmth; you look done in, lass.'

Luke looked at her as if he, too, had only just realised how tired she was. She had not slept for nearly twenty hours. Since that time she had walked, run, ridden, half starved, near frozen and finally found a little haven of warmth. It was enough to make her body demand sleep instantly. However, she smiled, professed she was fine and snuggled down into the chair.

'Now, lad, what brings you to my door?' Obadiah gestured that Luke use the stool, whilst he propped himself against a small barrel which he unearthed after removing a piece of oilskin that had covered it from view.

'I would always find my way to your door, wouldn't I?' Luke replied, rubbing his face with his hands while he leaned forward as if trying to fight off his own fatigue.

'Aye, that you would, but it never usually took you three seasons to do it before.' He sniffed. Florence thought that, although he was a hardened man, at least to the elements, there was a note of hurt in his voice.

'I only returned to my estate earlier this morning, Obadiah,' Luke said.

The man raised both brows so much that they almost disappeared from view under his hat. 'You are either taking Obadiah for an old fool, or you have had a serious fall off that nag of yours; you should have used a saddle. That manor house was opened up again nine months since and you is said to be living the life of the lord of the manor in it. No time for local folk, too busy reorganising your soldiers and making walls to keep either you in or honest folks well out.'

'I didn't see any new walls,' Florence commented.

'Some walls aren't made of brick or stone, miss,' the fisherman replied.

'It isn't me, Obe, it is an impostor, who resembles me in colouring and stature, but is no more a Stainbridge than you. I need to get him out and prove that I am Luke Stainbridge and I am back to stay. I want that blackguard to pay for what he has done to my staff, my home and property and to my good name.'

Florence thought to herself that the fact he had placed his staff before his own losses spoke loudly for the compassion of this strange man with whom she was rapidly becoming very familiar.

'I spent enough time in a French gaol, planning my joyful return, but it has not materialised. I need your help.' Through half-lidded eyes she saw the imploring look upon Luke's face.

'It is a fancy tale you tell me, but how do I know you is you and he is not? It is over six years since I've seen thee, and you was a boy back then and pale as the lass. Now you're a man growed with hard muscles and a tanned skin that make you look like a sea dog. Your hands are work-roughened now, unlike those of the soppy boy who had been doted on from birth.' The man shifted uneasily.

'Five years it has been, and how would he know your secret passwords? We played pirates in the dunes when I first discovered this place, and you scared me half to death. You were the first man of the sea I had ever been near and you taught me so much whenever my father was away in town.

We spent many hours together.

'How could you not know me for who I am, Obe? I bet he has not been near here once. So, how many of the old staff still work at the manor?'

The older man smiled and tossed Luke a bottle, which he opened. 'None, lad, the bas — ' he hesitated and glanced at Florence who had let her lids close whilst enjoying the warmth and listening to the men talk. 'The blighter brought foreigners in to man the house.'

'Foreigners?' Luke queried.

'Aye, from London and thereabouts. None of the locals live there now. He is even replacing the Captain of the militia in a few months. Josephus was well pi — ' he hesitated again, ' — really disappointed that he was not staying on. However, you — that is the Stainbridge man, who carries out the orders as if he was you, said he would be paid up until the end of his term, then someone from out of the county is coming in — another foreigner. People don't think on your name with kindness anymore, lad.' He sniffed again before adding, 'Your young lady has nodded off. Pretty thing, if you don't mind my sayin' so.'

'No, I don't mind you saying that at all, Obadiah. But I need to speak to this Josephus. If he can be trusted, I need his help.'

'He is a soldier — can they be trusted?'

The question hung in the air as Florence drifted off to sleep with a happy heart. Luke had not protested in the slightest at her being referred to as his young lady.

8

The captain returned to the garrison to find that he had a visitor waiting for him. He knew the carriage, he would not rush; it was the man who paid for his men to stable and billet on his land. The Stainbridge carriage was all nice and shiny, unlike the shabby vehicle he had taken Mrs Haggerty back to the school in. Josephus was in no mood to see the man. He had to show deference to him, but they had disliked each other on sight, and the captain knew that was why he had not been allowed to stay on.

He had built this force up under the loose supervision of Mr Archibald Stainbridge, when the younger, obnoxious cousin and rightful heir had taken himself off to pester Napoleon. It was a shame really that this 'lost' soul had found his way back from behind enemy lines, smelling sweet, as if he had lived his life in a boudoir not as a prisoner of an enemy. Still, the man had the decency not to dwell on his escape or release, and hardly ever bothered the captain. Josephus presumed he had recovered in London before taking up his rightful position here.

Yet, still, he missed Mr Archibald, a jovial sort of man. It was a blessing he had not bought a commission, for certainly he would have caused the death of his regiment. Instead he had apparently taken himself off to the spa in Harrogate before heading to London for a season of gaiety and theatre. His type looked upon war and Napoleon as an inconvenience that mere fighting men would see off.

Josephus stepped down from his dog-eared carriage and was pleased to see his sergeant instantly by his side. 'What news, Trivett?' he asked.

'His 'lordship' is drinking your finest brandy in your room, sir. He's in a vexed mood and not happy you was not here to greet him.' There was a twinkle in the sergeant's eyes. They had fought together in real wars and, unlike the rest of the men who were battle virgins, these two hardened campaigners knew a sop when they saw one.

'Oh, what a shame,' Josephus replied, without making any movement toward the stairs. 'But I actually meant, what news of the young lass?'

'Well, sir, that's a thing, because the only trail we picked up led toward the Stainbridge land itself. Looks like she came down the river on the back of a barge, the lad swears he had no knowledge of a stowaway and I believe him. Anyways she hopped off, taking the vale road. Now, I knows a lassy in the kitchens there called Sally. She ain't allowed off the estate and was brought in from the poorhouse at York. But I sometimes take a stroll through the grounds and happen across her when she is picking mushrooms and herbs or the like.'

Josephus looked at him impatiently. 'The short version, man!'

'Sorry, sir. She has said that she saw a man and a young lass riding out of the barn on a horse with only a bridle on. Stainbridge's men gave chase but lost them by the river. Then the asylum cart arrived, but the man had broken free and carried off the lassy.'

The captain stared at him in bewilderment.

'You cannot let slip the girl's name, sir, or she would be in danger, I'm sure. They keep a tight house up there.'

'Telling me what I can and can't do, Trivett?' the captain said as he mulled over what was being told to him.

'No, sir, just saying,' Trivett replied softly.

'Your bit of skirt is safe from me, I do not pass on gossip. What asylum cart and what man?' The captain was now talking with his voice lowered.

'Sal didn't know why they locked a man away, but they did. He'd come to the front of the house, the main door. She didn't hear what went on but said they dragged him back to a store room.

127

She said he was raving and they sent for the doctor from the asylum. There was a right kerfuffle. No one knew who the girl was or where she came from, but they both fled together and are being chased. I think that is why *he's* here.' He glanced up the stairs to the captain's office.

'Where is his ostler?' Josephus asked, glancing around them hoping he was not within earshot.

'We sent him to the stables; he said one of his horses has picked up a stone in its hoof. He wouldn't take a drink or say ought.' The man shrugged.

'Does he know about the missing girl?' Josephus asked.

'No, sir.' He stood tall. 'I was not encouraged to speak, so I said nought,' he answered, and risked a half smile.

'You did well. See that this man does not gossip to the other men. I shall find out what *he* wants.' He watched as his trusted friend and sergeant went to carry out his orders.

It was turning out to be an

interesting day. He climbed the stairs to his office, wondering if a woman with the presence and wit of Mrs Haggerty would really take on an old soldier, such as him, on a whim. Then he remembered the spark in her eyes, and how it had been masked and subdued once more when she had returned to the school and the leech of a man, Carrie, and decided there was every chance she would take his offer and decide to live again.

'Good God, man, how long does it take you to climb stairs? It is just as well you are retiring soon,' Stainbridge snapped without preamble as soon as the captain entered the room. 'Now sit down and listen to me. We have a situation. We have two fugitives at large and I want them both caught. The man is dangerous — a lunatic. Find him, dead or alive, before he kills the girl or anyone who crosses their path!'

The words came flooding out of the man's mouth in one vast tirade. Josephus shut the door behind him, turned to his unwelcome visitor and said calmly. 'Should we start at the beginning, sir? Put some sense and order into it.'

The man he knew as Mr Luke Stainbridge took in a deep breath of frustration and began to explain how a man had entered his home, ranted wildly and, when they had tried to apprehend him before he could do more damage, had escaped their grip and absconded with a wench.

Josephus' eyebrows creased. There was no mention of the man being locked up by them as the girl Sally had recounted to Trevitt. 'A servant wench?' he asked.

'Of course!' Stainbridge snapped.

'Of your staff?' he queried further.

'No . . . em, she was with him . . . his whore no doubt, most likely a wanton tavern girl. I want them both caught. He stole one of my horses.'

'Did he force this wench or was she a willing accomplice, sir?' The captain saw the annoyance in the other man's eyes.

'She shared the back of one of my horses with him willingly enough, flashing her legs for the world to see as they headed into the forest. We lost their trail in there. Find them and take them straight to the asylum. Do not listen to their rantings — and Captain, you shoot if you must. They are dangerous people, who would think nothing of hurting or killing innocent souls. They threatened me and attacked my men and my kitchen girl — he actually manhandled her!' He walked over to the doorway.

'Your servant girl?'

'Sally, a simple soul, but she does not deserve to be abused so. Hurry, darkness will fall soon. You must find them by morning, or no one will be safe. I want a guard of men around the manor and give them instructions to shoot them on sight if they return. Am I making myself clear?'

'Very, sir,' the captain replied, as he watched the man leave. *Some soldier you were,* he thought, *if you couldn't* track a girl and a man on a horse, bareback, in peace time across your own land. *No wonder that he has been a guest of the French,* he mused, *they would have seen him coming the moment he stepped off the ship.*

He rested against his desk and thought deeply as he listened to the carriage leave. 'Could it be the same girl? How did she hitch herself up with a madman who knew the land, and burst into the manor with such ease and so quickly? Was he an old acquaintance of her father's, or someone that Luke Stainbridge had wronged? Either way, they needed to find the man before Stainbridge's useless henchmen or he would never find the truth of it.

'What orders, sir?' Trevitt asked when he returned.

'Tell five of the men to guard the manor and apprehend anyone who tries to force their way in. Shoot only to maim, and only if necessary; I want to question them. Tell them to avoid shooting at all if they can and bring them back to me alive. My orders are to be kept secret. If anyone asks if clear orders have been given to them, they are to say their orders are very clear to them and no more.'

The sergeant turned to leave. 'George, you and I are going hunting tonight. We will need horses, pistols, possibly a lantern and some tethers. We shall not be back before morning, I fear. If the men find the girl, she is to be kept here in a cell until I return, not sent back to the school straight away. She is to be given blankets and food and treated well.'

'Yes, sir!' the man barked back.

Josephus grinned. His friend would be leaving with him in three months' time and had taken the invitation to be a gamekeeper on his land in Suffolk, but this interesting set of events was going to give them the chance to be proper soldiers once more, and they both knew it.

★   ★   ★

The two men set off as light was beginning to fade. They started by following the river from the opposite bank from where Stainbridge had said that his men had lost the trail. They moved downstream, then picked up a set of tracks by a bridge, which led them out of the forest onto the open road. The captain knew their hunt had begun. There, the tracks were lost and found again after some time and effort. From the barn they rode further across the vale till their path led to the old Norman church of St Oswald's. Here in the dark of night they found the church door had been opened and two sets of footprints were clearly discernible just inside the door. No attempt seemed to have been made to steal the church silver.

Trevitt paused by a pew. He bent down. 'Looks like they stopped for dinner,' he commented as he flicked a few crumbs to the floor. They looked to the vicarage; it was in darkness.

'No damage done, though, and

nothing taken,' he said as he looked at the collection box which was on the wall by the main doors. 'A thief with a conscience?'

'Do I rouse Mr Reedman?' Trevitt asked as they crossed from the church to the vicarage.

'No, that will take time.' They skirted around to the back of the vicarage, the captain nodded and Trevitt tried the door, which opened. He was going to enter, but the captain stopped him.

'No point, they've already left here. Check inside quickly and make sure no one is harmed, then we will continue if all is well. I do not expect to see any sign of a fight.'

The captain stared at the stars, wondering, trying to make sense of the pieces of unconnected information he had received. These two people seemed very connected . . . but how?'

'Cook's sleeping like a hog, if you know what I mean, sir — no one has disturbed her, but the larder door was open.'

135

'Good. We continue.' They walked their horses quietly around the grounds until the captain picked up the trail again. He gave one solitary low whistle; his sergeant mounted straight away and followed him. Now, by the light of a full moon, they followed the track which left the vale and headed east towards the coast.

'Where do we head? To Ebton?' Trevitt asked.

'To a man who sells excellent brandy and who knows these parts better than any. He will have to help us find these people so that we can resolve a puzzle quickly.' The captain looked at his friend.

'Obadiah don't like house calls, sir. Bad for his image,' Trevitt shouted as they galloped along the road.

'That's a coincidence, sergeant, as I don't like calling uninvited, but needs must, man, needs must. I will find that girl for Amelia Haggerty and if she has been compromised in any way I will skin this man's back myself, whoever he is.'

They rode on in silence, stopping only to rest at the inn in Ebton. They had to knock hard upon the door to wake Amos up, but when he saw the red jackets, he opened up without question.

However, each and every question they asked him whilst they ate and drank the man's food was greeted with a denial of knowledge or a nonchalant shrug. Josephus expected nothing less. They were a close-knit community of brigands, but he sheltered there for four hours until the daylight began to return and the search could continue in earnest.

Word would have reached Obadiah that they were looking for the girl and, the captain hoped, that it was he who was seeking her. Then his meeting with Obadiah would be sooner rather than later.

9

Florence slept soundly and awoke early when she heard movements around her. Glancing down at the floor by her chair, she saw Luke rousing himself. She was disorientated but a blast of wind chilled her as the door of the hut was opened wide, bringing her senses screaming into reality. Luke sprang up from where he had been sleeping peacefully, instantly alert. The weather-worn face of Obadiah Muckford greeted them harshly with words snapped out in a rush on the wind.

'I've heard from the villagers over Ebton that the militia have been combing the county for this lass.' He tossed a cob of bread to Luke, and a jug of milk he handed carefully to Florence. 'No cups here, lassy, just drink your fill from that and pass it to his lordship 'ere. Be quick, we need to get you out of here and safe away. They've told me two soldiers stayed all night in the inn waiting for you to turn up.'

'Why are the militia bothering to look for me? Why would I go to an inn? How do you know it is me they seek?' Florence's mind was a whirl with questions and indecision.

'Because you are Christopher Swan's girl if ever I saw the living image of him. They are searching for you, my dear, and we want to keep you safe. Your pa was one of us, and what they did to him was barbaric — present company excepted.' He looked at Luke.

'I need to find the captain you spoke of, Obe. Can you hide Florence away until it is safe for her to be seen once more?' Luke asked, glancing at her with a look of concern. The older man nodded his agreement.

Florence stood tall, though that was still quite short in comparison to Luke, fighting the feeling of panic within her. She didn't understand what was happening around her any more, but her heart told her head she had no wish to be separated from this man. 'You two seem to have forgotten something, gentlemen. I am not your chattel to do with as you wish. I have a mind and will of my own and where he goes, sirs, I go!' she declared.

Both men stared at her.

'See, I told you she's Swan's daughter!' Obadiah said gruffly. 'That's the same pig-headed outspoken spirit that got him transported. If he hadn't stayed to help Elijah land that last load of kegs, and then let rip into the Riding Officer he would never have been seen and recognised. 'Twas his downfall. Archibald was sorely hurt that he had to be a part of the — '

'That's enough blithering, man. Florence, it is enough that I have men out searching for me. If the whole militia is out looking for a lost woman, you will only attract more trouble and attention which will make my quest more difficult, if not impossible. Can you not see that?'

'Yes, I see very clearly, and that makes you a coward, sir!'

Luke's head jerked around to face her as Florence spoke her words of defiance. A second of silence hung in the air; even the wind seemed to still.

'Eeh, lassy, the mouth on you is worse than that of your old man. See what happens when a woman gets schooled.' Obadiah shook his head and stared back out of his hut, scouring the dunes for signs of life.

'Is that what you truly think of me?' Luke was staring at her, the intensity made her feel awkward.

'You only worry that I bring danger to you, yet I was the one who helped you to find your cousin Mr Archibald.'

'You found Mr Archibald?' Obadiah interjected.

'Yes,' Luke said distractedly, as he held Florence's accusing stare. 'I am worried for your safety, Florence. I thought that if I could convince you that coming with me jeopardised *my* safety then you would agree to stay. I obviously made a misjudgement.'

'Where is he, then?' Obadiah asked.

'Like the one your family made against my father, apparently! You said that, didn't you?' She stared at Obadiah.

'Yes, sort of. It's the job of the magistrate to catch law-breakers. The older Mr Archibald hated the trade and any who gained by it.' The fisherman shook his head as if he couldn't comprehend the man's thinking, then looked at Stainbridge. 'Where is young Mr Archibald?' he repeated, becoming impatient with the fragmented conversation they were having.

'If you stay with me, you must do what I say and when, or else you risk both our freedoms. I am no coward, Miss Swan!'

'That's nice, you two stand here and fight it out, whilst them soldiers make their way up the beach to search here. Well, I've me livelihood to think of, and unless you take that nag of yours and clear off to the old farm and wait for me there, then no one is going to find the captain or help you and your cousin Mr Archibald!' The man's voice bellowed around the hut like the gusts of wind outside.

Both Luke and Florence stared at him, then quickly and silently left the shelter of his hut.

★   ★   ★

Luke helped Florence onto the horse, jumped up behind and rode as if they were being chased by the devil. He kept a strong arm around her and she curved into his body and clung to his arm, holding the animal as tightly as she could with her thighs.

Eventually she managed to make herself heard. 'Luke, stop, please!'

He slowed down, turned to make sure that they were not being followed and walked the horse towards a ramshackle stone building with a broken cart propped against its wall. It was deserted and a good half mile off the track that served as a coastal road.

The wind howled over the land, sweeping over the headland ahead of them. The vantage point here looked down across a sweeping bay. An unruly sea crashed beneath, gulls squawked high above and, although windswept and deserted, this stone relic continued to exist, even as the land fell away slowly over years, eating into what was once its farmland.

He walked the horse into the open end of the building where once a roof covered the whole space. Tethered there by the reins, it soon settled. Without speaking; he then entered the main part of the cottage. Florence followed. She could sense a quiet rage brooding within the man.

Once inside, he moved dusty stools around, threw off an old piece of sheeting that covered a small chest and looked at her, wild and dishevelled as she appeared. He gestured to her to sit upon the stool. Then after checking outside again, returned to open the chest. He had removed the bag which had been slung over his shoulder since they had left the manor.

Opening it, he withdrew a pistol. Florence watched as he opened the chest. Inside were the supplies needed to make the weapon ready for use: powder, shot, oil and cloths. There was also a small bottle of vinegar and some larger strips of cloth.

This Florence realised, was a place where the hunted could come to hide or prepare for a battle, possibly with the Riding Officers. It was perhaps where her father had run to and been caught. She knew little of why he had left her at the forge in the care of a neighbour one day; he said a brief and tearful goodbye to her. It all happened so quickly, with no explanation; he had just said he had to go, that men would come, but she was not to think ill of him, no matter what people said once he had gone. He had left, and she had been bundled off to a school, not knowing where 'gone' was.

Her only information of what had become of him had been told to her by Mrs Haggerty, who had proclaimed him to be sent to the colonies for being a thief. No mention was made of what became of the forge, or his possessions. Florence still remembered the stab of pain the news had caused, and the fact that she had been given merely an hour to compose herself before being obliged to begin her work.

That day she had discovered the true meaning of loneliness, a feeling which had stayed with her until this adventure had begun. Now, looking at Luke, she realised she did not want to be lonely any more.

'Why are you so angry?' she asked.

'I am no coward!' he repeated, without even looking up at her. Instead, he continued to clean his gun.

She knelt by him, placing a hand gently over his, as he held the pistol. 'I'm sorry. I spoke irrationally, careless words spoken purely out of fear.'

'Exactly my point!' he snapped. 'You

have every right to be scared, but I could have made sure that you were safe. My fight here is dangerous.'

'No, you misunderstand me. I spoke out because I was afraid of being separated from you. If we stay together, we can both stay safe, I know it.'

He placed the gun and cloth on the floor and held her shoulders so that she had to look at him directly.

'Florence, you hope so. You may even plan it so, but that does not mean it will be. If the man in the manor is believed and I cannot force an investigation into his legality before being thrown into an institution, then I am doomed. The doctor will be in his pay; as many a recruiting sergeant knows, it is possible that their professional judgement can be bought. Then my plight will be dire.

'I have no wish to drag an innocent woman there with me. They would break you, Florence, and that I could not bear. You need to stay free with your dreams and ideals. Stay free, let

Obadiah see you safe, and do not look back. If I manage to restore my lands to myself then you will have a life free of care, and that I can promise you.'

'Would it be in your home, though, with you?' she asked, and felt her cheeks burn at her forward question. 'As your housekeeper?'

He glanced over his shoulder before letting his eyes find hers. The moment he took her into his arms, they both surrendered to the emotion; their embrace felt natural, each clinging to the other as if each breath, each touch and every kiss could be their last.

A warm feeling swept through her body — her senses heightened, aware of his touch as his hands stroked her back, pulling her in to his muscular, solid frame. He uttered a low groan, holding her firmly in his arms, and tilted his head upwards as he hugged her to him for a long moment before finally he pulled away.

'Stop now, Florence. We must — ' He cleared his throat. 'This is too soon for you and certainly not the best of times for . . . This is wrong. We do not think straight. We are fugitives, and I should know better.' He stepped away. 'I apologise. I must finish making the pistol ready.'

'But, Luke, we . . . '

'No, Florence, we must watch each others' backs and think only of surviving this ordeal. The future is, as yet, not ours to see, and our intimacy is moving too fast. You must keep watch.' He barked out the last comment as an order which she obeyed.

He was wrong. Her body, she knew, was more than ready for his touch. Time, place, social standing all laughed in her face. For here was a man she trusted, admired and wanted. He a gentleman and she a runaway maid. What freedom did she ever hope to find beyond the freedom to act as she willed with a man she felt safe with? Time meant nothing to her, so long as they could be together.

Florence had fallen in trouble again,

but this time it had led her to a great desire — not just for one of her plans to be fulfilled, but for her body to be. She had fallen quickly and deeply in love.

10

Mr Reedman entered the manor to be escorted to the library by Esher, the manservant of the new master of the house. He was announced and entered holding his black hat in his hand, showing a grey, thinning head of shoulder-length hair. The doors were shut firmly behind him.

'Now, Reedman, what news do you have for me?' The man stepped forward to greet the slightly-built clergyman. His smile was affable and, with a friendly arm placed around the dour man's shoulders, he steered his visitor over to the warmth of a fire and seated him in one of two chairs by the marble hearth.

'Not much in the way of news, sir. Mr Archibald seems quite comfortable. Your good doctor gives him his medication regularly, he asks about you and the manor occasionally, between the occasional trauma. He still has the odd nightmare, but then when he has his medicine, he is happy again. His nerves could not cope with the responsibility of the estate, you were correct, sir. It must have been the trauma and shock of your absence and then you coming home a hero, fit and well. He will settle again, sir, given time. He is, I understand, a sensitive man.'

'Yes, he is. I aim to get him the very best of help, Mr Reedman, which is why I have sent for you.' He smiled.

'Good, I am pleased to hear it.'

'Have you or Mr Archibald had any visitors?' he asked innocently.

'Funny you should ask that, sir. We thought there was vermin in our larder last night as some victuals had been tampered with. However, a bottle of Mr Archibald's best vintage had disappeared too, and it turned out to be a couple of soldiers. They didn't wake Cook up, but sneaked in and out without a by-your-leave. If they had roused her when they came in she'd have screamed the place down, but she woke feeling the draught from the door — I reprimanded her for forgetting to lock and bolt it. When she looked out, there was two militia men riding off.

'I do think, sir, you could have words with the captain about such cavalier behaviour from his men. Makes us feel violated, like we're not safe in our beds from our own protective officers. What they did, sir, was common theft and trespass.' He sniffed, affronted.

'Yes, of course, I shall indeed. You are certain they did not trespass further?' he pushed.

'Absolutely, Cook is as good as a hound. She'd have turned them out if they'd tried to pass her, sir. No — Mr Archibald was as safe as houses.'

'That is as may be. Although it is sooner than I had anticipated, I fear that I and dear Mr Archibald will be returning to London. Some unexpected business has come up and I have decided to close up the manor. It has been my intention to have him seen by the best physician I can find in London, since my reappearance has caused him to have such a turn. I will see that his nerves are restored to health.'

The Reverend looked a little puzzled. 'Close up, sir? Isn't it a little early in the season to be doing that? Grouse will be good this year and — '

'Mr Reedman, I will be closing the manor — and selling it, and the land, as soon as I return to London.'

The Reverend gasped. 'But what of the tenants, the militia . . . ?'

'I have thought about these people, of course. The militia will not be disbanded or discarded. The nation's security is always at my heart. The tenants will be found a new and reasonable squire and I shall see the church is compensated against any hardship it may suffer in the short term. I may even apportion a piece of land to be entrusted to it.' He smiled reassuringly.

'I am sure you will look after the local interests as your good father did before you and Mr Archibald lived here.' Mr Reedman looked nervous and unsure as he wrung his hands in his lap. It was clear he did not feel all was well with this new plan that he was being presented with.

'Mr Reedman, I want you to accompany my cousin to an address I will give you in London. He is to be cared for there. I fear the air up here is too rare for him.'

'If you'll excuse me saying so, sir, it may be rare but it is a lot cleaner than the fetid air of the city.' His words were surprisingly direct.

'I do agree, which is why he will only be going to have prescribed treatment and then he will need to be taken on to a much gentler climate where he can visit a spa. Perhaps Bath — Aqua Sulis. The waters are said to be extremely kind to the nerves.

'Of course I will pay all your expenses, including the stipend you will pay a curate to cover your duties for your absence, and of course the running of your home whilst you are away. I suspect a month's expenses should cover the needs for a week's trip. Do you agree?'

The Reverend's mouth hung open. 'It is very sudden; these things usually take time to arrange. I had promised to visit — '

'Name your fee, and I shall double it and all will be ready to go in two days, sir. Will it not?' His smile faded while he watched the man's eyes; he had him, he would believe his lies, because he had named the price of this man's soul.

Mr Reedman nodded reluctantly. 'Yes, I think it can be arranged.'

'Good,' he said calmly, leaning forward towards the bewildered clergyman. 'Some people will be upset by my decision and may cause a fuss. I need your discretion here. Do not say what I intend to do with the estate, but instead, let it just be known you are accompanying a weak soul to a physician in London. That way you tell no lies.'

'Of course, sir, of course,' he said. 'How could I do any other?'

'You may go, but be ready in two days' time. I will send a vehicle early, at daybreak. Have him ready.'

Mr Reedman bowed slightly before leaving. Esher showed him out and then returned to the library; a crooked smile upon his lips gave him a sinister expression. 'He seemed happy enough, sir?'

'He is. Every man has a price, particularly if they don't realise the ultimate one is their life. You will leave here tomorrow, Esher. When he has delivered Archibald to the address, you pay him off. Make sure you see him put the purse in his pocket and then you follow him and — oh, dear — another murderous, cowardly attack upon a man of God will mar the streets of London. Make sure you do not leave any address or paper on him which can carry a trail back to here. We will need to sell the deeds of this place quickly and vanish to Bristol as soon as we drain off the London accounts.'

'Yes, sir.' He turned to go but hesitated. 'What of Mr Archibald?'

'Once he has been with me to the bank, in as near a sober state as we can get him, we leave him in one of the opium houses, see he has his share and walk away. He has no sense when he is clear-headed, so by the time he has partaken of the drug and they realise he has no more money or friends they'll strip him and Mother Thames will have a bigger fish to play with. He won't be a problem; he has never been to the city and we won't have done a thing. We'll be on board a ship by then.

'A new life beckons, Esher. I was bored here, anyway.'

11

The flat sandy bay swept away from the dunes, passing the fishing villages of Ebton and Seaham as it ended on the horizon, dominated by the headland of Stangcliffe. Obadiah breathed the salty air, felt its moisture upon his face and stroked his dampened beard. He loved this place. He saw the riders long before they reached him. It was what made the place so perfect — remote, yet accessible, if you knew the tides and the rocks.

He reached his boat as they neared him. 'Sir, what brings you all the way out to this cold place?' Obadiah called out, as he leaned over his coble, which was beached near the shoreline.

The captain and Trevitt had ridden over to him when they saw Obadiah crossing from the dunes, walking through the soft sand, then onto the firmer wet shoreline to his boat. That had given his unwanted guests the time they needed to leave his hut unnoticed by the militia. However, when he saw that the soldiers his over-excited friends had told him about were none other than the captain and Trevitt, Obadiah realised he should have let them be. No one had said that the soldiers in the inn were they.

Sometimes, he thought in exasperation, he felt as if he was surrounded by men with heads full of oakham instead of their God-given brains. He had to organise the whole lot of them, think for them, plan and plot so that they didn't end up like Elijah and Swan.

'A runaway lass and a madman. Have you seen either, Obadiah, for I need to be the first to find them?' The captain was looking up and down the beach as he spoke, then his eyes settled on Obadiah.

Obadiah threw a rope which he had carried down to the beach into his coble and then slowly turned to the captain, whom he had known for three years since he stumbled across him with a stash of kegs.

The captain, he knew too well, was also was capable of thinking things out. The result had been that he had gained a regular supply of brandy, and Obadiah had moved most of his operation beyond the captain's jurisdiction. It was an arrangement which had worked well, but now change was on its way, unless Obadiah foiled the impostor at the manor and in so doing protected the status quo. That was a term he had learned from the young Stainbridge lad, many summers since.

'I don't know about a runaway lass, but I surely haven't seen a madman around these parts. But a wronged one . . . now, I could say yes to that for sure.' He leaned against the coble and looked up at the captain. He was taking a risk, but he was a man who was used to that.

'A wronged one, like you, finding him with kegs and been accused by a

161

stranger of hiding them?' Josephus asked. Trevitt sneered.

'No — much worse, far worse. Wronged as in his land and home have been taken from him by someone who claims to be him. The man is running without the ability to get to the folk he can trust and prove who he is.'

Trevitt laughed openly. 'He is mad, then,' he declared.

'No, sir, that he is not, because I've known him as a boy and he is that same boy who has turned into the man grown.

'The man you are chasing is the real Mr Luke Stainbridge and he is being hunted from his home by a stranger who runs his own soldiers — your good self and the militia who follow. He needs help, sir, to get him back to where he should be. The man who claimed to be him, who is living his life, has had him labelled mad and so he has had to go to ground before the impostor's doctor declares him mad and drugs him up.'

'Where is he?' the captain asked urgently.

'He needs help.' Obadiah approached the captain's horse.

'If what you say is true, then I will help him,' the captain said. 'But why has he taken the girl?'

Obadiah laughed. 'You got that wrong, too, sir. I think the lass has tagged on to him. She's a pretty thing, too.'

The captain placed a hand on Obadiah's shoulder. 'Has he taken advantage of a foolish young woman?'

'No, not Mr Luke. He's keeping her safe.' Obadiah looked at the captain's stirrup. 'Unhook yer foot from there and give an old fisherman a hike up, then and I'll show you where they are, but I'm thinking we'll stop before we go forward, as it's best he sees Obadiah first before them pretty red jackets of yours, eh?'

With a heave and a pull Obadiah was seated behind the captain and they headed as quickly as the sand and the

163

heavy load would allow the horse to travel, back through the dunes to the track that led to the old farm.

★ ★ ★

Florence watched Luke, as he in turn stared out of the cottage window. She realised she should never have called him a coward. He was brave, she could see that. A lesser man would have taken advantage of her situation or run screaming at the injustice of his home being overtaken by Luke II. Her thoughts, however, were interrupted, as he turned away from the window and faced her.

'If they are not here by noon, Florence, then I will take you to Newcastle. We will make haste and from there we will take a journey by ship or collier, whatever vessel we can buy passage on, to go straight to London. Many vessels a day make the journey; it would take time for us to be tracked and our destination discovered.

'Once there, I will be able to prove

who I am to the authorities and protect at least some of my assets. However, I fear it will be too late to apprehend the blackguard at the manor, for he will know I have slipped away to regain control of my life. He will be planning to leave with whatever he can manage to steal whilst he is at liberty to do so. The man has no shame and heaps of confidence, as the best of conmen have.

'But I will make sure you are safe, Florence. Never fear.' He walked over and put a protective hand upon her shoulder.

'What will you do, sir? Find me a position working as a maid for one of your gentlemen friends?' She had no idea what possessed her to speak so to him, other than the thought that once he returned to London, he would be a 'someone' and she would be a 'no one' again. It was a thought that stuck in her throat and pierced her vulnerable heart.

He shook his head at her. 'One minute you are as sweet as a little kitten, the next as wild as a full-grown minx! You have a mouth on you, as Obadiah said. I was trying to reassure you, woman!'

'Of what, though? That you are a class apart, that you are a gentleman? Can you not see, as you so elegantly showed me in the barn, my plan, my dream, my life's hopes rested upon ignorance?

'A person cannot cross the divides of class. A woman cannot survive without a man's protection, because men have made it so. You are a man, Luke, but I am not a good enough woman to be seen with you in London.' Her voice had become vexed as she spoke and her conviction grew with each word.

He smiled at her, and then took a step back whilst he peered out of the window again. Once he was certain that no one approached, he placed the pistol upon the table and came to her, tenderly taking hold of her roughened hands in his.

'I will secure my estate. I will involve the authorities. I will send word to your school that you are safe and not return-ing to them or the mill. You will be good enough stock to live in the manor here. You can see what it is like to live as a lady would. I will have you taught manners and etiquette, improve your letters, play an instrument, embroider . . . '

'I know well enough how to embroider and make lace. You are making a fool of me. You are cruel, Luke Stainbridge. You laugh at my ignorance while you have your knowledge of the world; you have become cynical of it and killed off a girl's dreams. That is so cruel,' she said sadly, looking down at her delicate hands within the strength of his rough ones.

Before he could answer, the distant sound of riders took his attention. He picked up the pistol, upturned the table and told Florence to curl up behind it, whilst he took up a place to the side of the window.

'Who is it?' Florence whispered.

'Militia. Stay quiet; do not scream as they enter.' He stood to the side of the doorway with his pistol raised ready to strike.

167

12

Florence heard voices and wanted to help Luke if the men burst in to overpower him. She saw a rusty iron poker by the old hearth, and instantly a plan formed in her mind of how she could strike. It had obviously been used at some time to tend the fire, and then discarded like the cottage. She reached for it, grasping it tightly, and balanced carefully upon her haunches. As soon as anybody attacked Luke, she would pounce. They were in this together — although she didn't know what exactly it was, because the militia should be the people that Luke could turn to for help.

Then she wondered if he was only fighting them because he was with her. If they were looking for her, then it was nothing to do with his problem at the manor. It could be simply because he had been seen riding off with her. She clung to the poker, thinking ruefully that all she had done since leaving the school was make a muddle into a complete mess.

Obadiah approached the door. 'Mr Stainbridge . . . Mr Luke, it is I. I have brought the captain to you and his sergeant. There is no need for a fight. They want to help you both.'

Florence peeped around the table and saw Luke peeking through the door jamb. He lowered his pistol, gesturing that she should stay hidden. But she stood up and boldly shouted to Obadiah, 'I am here on my own and I'm coming out.'

Luke rolled his eyes to the ceiling; she had annoyed him again, but she thought it was for his own good. Before she could do anything else, however, Obadiah stepped inside, glancing to Luke as he did.

'If you're not going to shoot me, lad, I'll introduce you to a friend — a much-needed one.' He took the poker from Florence and told her, 'You, lass, need a good hiding. You might have your father's spirit but tha' common sense is one bucket short of a pail!'

She opened her mouth to protest but the appearance of the two soldiers in the old cottage made her step back beside Luke and keep quiet. She could not see how to help. Every time she tried, she made matters worse.

'Good day, sir. I am Captain Josephus Brent and this is Sergeant Trivett. I understand you are the real Luke Stainbridge.'

He stood before Luke and offered him his hand.

'Yes, I am,' Luke replied confidently, and placed the pistol upon the righted table that Obadiah had lifted. 'I would be obliged if you and your men could help me to liberate my cousin from where he is being kept incarcerated in a stupefied state, drugged by laudanum and dulled of senses. Then, I would like you to accompany me to my home where I would turn out the man who is claiming my birthright.' He smiled at Florence.

'Explain to me first how this young woman has come to be careering around the countryside with you.' The captain stared at her.

'She is in my care. Miss Swan left an establishment, Benford Mill School, which purports to be an educational charity helping young women prepare for work in their main mill, but I have come to understand that some of the young girls are found employment of a different sort elsewhere.

'Obadiah has details of a young woman who seems to have taken up many positions against her will, after being left at an inn on the outskirts of York. He told me about her last night, whilst Miss Swan slept.

'Miss Swan ran away to the safety — or so she thought — of the manor house, hoping to find someone to help, as she was uncertain of her friend's plight. Our paths crossed by chance and I have sworn to keep her safe and

171

have the school investigated, once my own dilemma has been resolved.'

Florence was tempted to call out, 'Liar!' but she knew he had lied, very convincingly, to protect her name, reputation and highlight the plight of her friend. Anger rose within her. The girls at the school had little knowledge of the outside world and trusted Mr Carrie. When he told them they would be found a happy place, a good employer who was kind, they followed him as they left the school — lambs to the slaughter.

She realised she was being spoken to by the captain. 'Miss?'

'Sorry, sir, what?' she replied as she saw all the men staring at her.

'Is this the truth, Miss Swan?' The captain stood before her. 'You do not have to lie to protect anyone.'

'This man has told you the truth. I planned to go to the manor. I was foolish and incredibly naive. I should have run to you, sir, but I feared that if I did then you would just send me back. I met Mr Stainbridge by chance when he broke out of the room they held him in. He isn't mad, sir.'

'Very well, I will believe you. I will also believe you, sir, as there is much that has not felt right about the new owner of the manor.'

'Then may I suggest we make haste to the manor?' urged Luke. 'Archibald is not in a fit state to ride; therefore to move him they will need to use a coach which will make their journey slow, so we will be able catch up with that. Let us arrest the impostor before he flees.'

'I have men protecting him.' The captain smiled. 'A force already waiting for us, strong enough to overpower his men.'

'Good! We waste no more time, then. I want to know who this blackguard is. I want to find out how he ever thought he could get away with this charade,' Luke growled, picking up his pistol. 'Obadiah, can Florence stay with you until I return?'

Florence was going to object but

Obadiah held her arm, firmly but gently tucked under his arm. 'Aye, sir. She'll be as safe as houses with me.'

The men mounted the horses outside the cottage. Florence stood next to Obadiah. She wanted to shout out, 'Take care,' but remained silent.

The captain rode over to her. 'Miss Swan, tell me something, honestly.'

'If I can I will, sir,' she replied curiously.

'Mrs Haggerty, did she treat you and the girls ill?'

Florence wondered why he should ask about old Haggerty, but she answered as honestly as she could. 'No, not really. I suppose she was what you would call 'firm but fair'. We knew the rules, and if we stayed within them we never felt her cane.'

The man nodded as he considered her words. Luke was anxious to be away and was already on his horse and four paces down the track. He had not made any attempt to speak to her. She knew where his heart was. They had been as equal only so long as he had no manor to call his own.

'One last question, Miss Swan. Did Mrs Haggerty have anything to do with preparing the girls that Mr Carrie took to other places than the mill?'

'Heavens, no, sir! She's as straight as a die. She wouldn't tolerate that. She was just gullible, like the rest of us. What the Beadle and Mr Carrie said was law. Not questioned, just obeyed.'

'Very well. Thank you for your honesty, Miss Swan. I assure you that I will see that it is rewarded.'

'Sir,' Florence said, stopping him as he was about to turn the horse away. He raised a quizzical brow.

'Please look after Mr Luke. I fear that man at the manor would have him killed to silence him.'

The captain smiled, nodded at her and then galloped away with the other two leaving her and Obadiah with a windswept walk back down to the fishermen's huts.

'No use setting your heart on that

one, lass, he is too high born for thee.'
Obadiah offered the advice she did not
want to hear.

'I have no intention of it!' she said,
annoyed with herself for being so
transparent in her affections.

'It is a long walk back,' he commented.

'Good!' she snapped.

'Ah, a lassy that wants a healthy
complexion and not one of those pasty
sops that the likes of him want.'

'It will give us time to talk,' she
explained.

'Now what would you like to talk
about?' he asked.

'My father. You implied you knew
him well,' she said with determination,
'and I would like to know him better.'

Obadiah turned to walk on. 'To know
him, lass, you only have to look into
your own heart.'

'The truth, not platitudes!' she
snapped wearily.

The fisherman stopped and looked at
her. He sighed, grunted and then began

to recount the stories of his old friend.

Florence followed in step, enthralled, hanging on the man's every word. She had dreamed of such an opportunity, but never thought to meet anyone who knew him well. Whether Obadiah exaggerated her father's best qualities or not, she listened — and for those precious hours, thoughts of Luke slipped from her mind, as pride and hope that her father might one day return to her were restored.

★   ★   ★

Luke and the captain arrived back at the barracks with their prisoner trussed up on the back of the horse Luke had been accused of stealing.

He had come relatively quietly. His man had already left an hour earlier and men had been sent to capture him. The Reverend had also been brought in for questioning and Archibald was being looked after by another doctor, who grimly foretold dark days while he was weaned off his regular dose of the addictive drug. However, Luke promised to help nurse his unfortunate cousin through the days and nights of hell that would follow. He would see Archibald returned to his senses.

The impostor was dragged into a cell. Luke grabbed him and slammed him against the stone wall. The captain watched, arms folded, as Luke ordered him to tell the truth or he would spend time in the asylum being treated as a madman who thought himself lord of the manor. The fear in the man's eyes had been complete.

'You were an officer. You never looked at your men as people, just as expendable creatures. Cannon fodder! Oh, I watched you, sir.

'You see, one of the men, when drunk, thought I was you.

'It was then that I thought about it. What if you went missing? What if, after a skirmish, you didn't go back, but eventually I did, in your place, as you? I wondered if it could be done. So when the opportunity arose, I did it. If the Frenchies had killed you as I thought they would, all the land would have stayed mine.' The man smiled, but Luke's fist wiped the grin from his face before he turned away in disgust.

'Leave him to the law, it will be harsh enough, sir,' the captain urged, and Luke nodded. He had heard and seen enough. No wonder the man had seemed familiar; he had fought alongside him. But it was his blow, and not the Frenchman's bullet, that had placed him behind enemy lines.

'Despicable coward!' he shouted at the crumpled man. 'Captain, you may stay on in your post, if you wish. I will not ask you to leave.'

The captain smiled. 'Well now, that is excellent news because I have begun courting, sir, and I would like to stay around here a while longer.'

Luke smiled, left and mounted his horse. He knew he had to return to Archibald — but first he had someone to collect.

★   ★   ★

When Luke came within sight of the fisherman's hut, Florence's face lit up. He had remembered her, after all!

'Obadiah, all is well. I shall send you something for your troubles,' he shouted, and the fisherman nodded before returning to his boat.

Luke slipped off his horse, embracing Florence as she ran up to him.

'I need your help, Florence. You always believed me. I need a friend I can trust.' He pulled her close but after a fleeting kiss on her cheek, Luke drew back and looked into her eyes.

'A friend?' she queried.

'In time, we will find the depth of that friendship, but for now you have a lot to learn. I have a cousin to help. We have all of our lives before us, and I would very much like you to be a part of that. Will you?'

Her arms encircled his neck; her lips found his, her eyes closed as she savoured the sensation of his passion as their kissed lingered, oblivious to all else. She felt his hands take hold of her waist as he lifted her bodily and swung her up into the saddle of the waiting horse.

'Mr Luke . . .'

'No, Florrie, just Luke between you and I. You will be yourself and I will learn to live again, seeing life afresh through your eyes.'

He stepped into the stirrup and swung up behind her. She squeezed his arm as he held her firmly. She had dared to dream and had planned a new life for herself — but she had never dreamed that her plans would work out so well, or that she would find someone so dear to share them with.

THE END

We do hope that you have enjoyed reading this large print book.

Did you know that all of our titles are available for purchase?

We publish a wide range of high quality large print books including:
Romances, Mysteries, Classics
General Fiction
Non Fiction and Westerns

Special interest titles available in large print are:
The Little Oxford Dictionary
Music Book, Song Book
Hymn Book, Service Book

Also available from us courtesy of Oxford University Press:
Young Readers' Dictionary
(large print edition)
Young Readers' Thesaurus
(large print edition)

For further information or a free brochure, please contact us at:
Ulverscroft Large Print Books Ltd.,
The Green, Bradgate Road, Anstey,
Leicester, LE7 7FU, England.
Tel: (00 44) **0116 236 4325**
Fax: (00 44) **0116 234 0205**

SONG OF MY HEART

Margaret Mounsdon

Andi Cox lands her dream job, looking after the two daughters of pop music icon Jas Summers. But when Jas starts arranging a summer charity concert in the grounds of his country house and the girls become the subject of kidnap threats, her troubles really begin . . . Along the way Andi acquires a new stepmother in the eccentric Hermione — and then she loses her heart to Jas . . .

TANGO AT MIDNIGHT

Cara Cooper

Nicci Tate has to play the part of entrepreneur to persuade bank manager Grant Blake to agree a loan. This would make her dream of opening her own shop come true. However, Nicci has demons in her past which could jeopardise everything — including Grant's growing fondness for her — and she cannot let him get too close. But Grant, who has a problem with theft at the bank and his own dark mystery, isn't a man who's easily turned away.